The Captain's Love

Ravenswood Series

Book 1

Beverly Kovatch

Dedication

I hope that all of you enjoy my newest series, and the journey that it takes you on.

To all my friends and family:

For once in my life I am doing something for myself that I totally enjoy. I couldn't have done it without all of your support

Prelude

The waves broke against the ship. They were as ravaging as he could ever remember them. The men were beginning to panic.

"Pull the sails down before the storm rips them to shreds," the captain screamed out trying to be heard over the thunder that was cracking in the angry black sky. The blue waves of the ocean were a formidable enemy. He watched carefully for the light that would tell him he was almost home.

Mary would not be waiting for him upon his return. She never worried when he was gone in fact he thought perhaps she enjoyed too much his time away. Their marriage was nothing but a sham.

Something their parents had contrived as a way to become even wealthier than they already were.

Outside of a few drunken sprees on both their parts, there was no love lost between the two of them.

Lizzie however was something quite different. She was beautiful, her long dark curly hair circled around her face. She would wait at the dock for every return of the ship. She would carry a basket of bakery for all the men as they departed the ship. It was Lizzie that made coming home a desire in his heart.

He was bringing treasures from India this time. The load would bring much wealth to all of them providing he could get the ship to ride out this storm. With this kind of wealth he could go anywhere, hide from the life he dreaded.

"Maybe we should lighten our load Captain?" The first mate said begging the Captain for fear the weight of their cargo would be the death of them all.

"No Mr. Carson, we will not lighten our load until I say so."

"Yes, sir" he responded directly as he shouted out orders to the rest of the crew. They all knew if they didn't make it to the protection of the cove soon they would perish in the storm.

They were faithful to the Captain though and followed his orders unquestionably. The storms raging waves did not distract the Captain for one moment. His thoughts were focused on returning safely to Lizzy.

His precious Lizzy, unlike his wife, would surely be waiting anxiously for his return. His trip had been delayed which angered him, but she told him she had something important to tell him. She seemed anxious, when he left that day, but told him the news could wait until he returned. He regretted now that he had put her off.

If Smiley hadn't told him there was a crack in the boom he could have spent the time she needed. He regretted the way that he put her off that day.

The six week voyage had turned into six months and he had a sense of foreboding that he could not shake.

He couldn't wait to see her beautiful face smiling back at him when he stepped off the ship. She would surely be on the dock in anticipation.

He thought of all the wasted years with Mary. It was only Matthew that meant everything from their vows. His father had forced him into this loveless marriage. This time it was over. He would not allow his father to keep him from his love.

He would rid himself of Mary, take Matthew and travel off with his beloved Lizzy. With the riches he brought back he, Lizzy, and Matthew could travel the world and never return to Ravenswood Manor.

The men were soaked by the waves of the storm but the light was just ahead.

“We’re home men. We made it to the light.” They were all shouting as the ship pulled into the cove.

The Captain jumped from the ship to the dock not even waiting for the gang plank to be laid out, but Lizzy wasn’t there and his heart felt fear for the first time.

Chapter One

“Come on Catherine, what do you mean they have another set of edits they want me to do on the book? Castaway Cove is perfect just the way it is.” She sighed out of aggravation. “By the time they get done with it there won’t be a word of what I originally wrote.”

“I know Ali, but this is what they want and if they are producing it you have to give them what they want.”

“Alright Cat, I will rewrite … again.” “I think we need to look at other publishers though. I seem to spend more time in rewrites than when I come up with the original story.”

“I swear Ali; this should be the last of the edits. Remember this is important and don’t forget. I set you up with a very important book tour in New England a week from Monday.”

"Yeah, yeah a book tour, how lovely. Now I have to call Eddie to get me a car rental and book me in the local hotel." She mumbled as she hung up the phone.

"Can you get me Eddie Danner please?" she says nonchalantly talking to her cell phone.

"Hey Eddie, Its Ali, can you get me booked in a hotel close to Bosh Bookstore somewhere around New Haven? Yes, that is Connecticut. Cat says that is centrally located to where all these stores are for this new book tour. Can you book me a rental car too? I think I am going to drive this time instead of fly. Thanks Eddie, you're a doll catch ya later."

Ali got off the subway with her suitcase in hand. She slung the briefcase that contained her laptop over her shoulder and started looking for a cab.

Travel was all she ever seemed to do anymore.

It was great for her book sales, but sometimes she just wanted to spend some time with her boyfriend Joe. They shared a small apartment just south of 5th street. It wasn't great but then the rent was reasonable for two people just starting out.

Meeting Joe had been a God send at the time. She was fresh out of college and had high hopes of being a famous writer. Joe was in construction and the local tavern was the place that they both hung out. The bar had free Wi-Fi so Ali would go there and sit in the back to write while he caroused with his friends. The cost of internet was too expensive and not quite on her budget so meeting and then having Joe share the cost of the apartment most certainly helped. Their personalities were quite different though. She was quiet and more withdrawn while he was loud and boisterous. He had friends galore while she had none. With the apartment being so small it was hard sometimes to concentrate on writing.

He would blast the game on TV, invite all his buddies over for a game party where they would all drink and carry on.

Joe was the kind of guy that liked to have fun, almost all the time actually, not to say she didn't but with all the book tours and traveling going on she liked to just come home to a glass of wine and silence. If it wasn't listening to his woes of how she always leaves him alone, it was party central with all his cronies.

He wasn't expecting her for another day so this was going to be a great surprise for him she thought. She had a bottle of sparkling wine that a bookstore owner gave to her to celebrate the success of her newest hit book. This would be the perfect ending, a quiet night alone to celebrate with Joe. She would set out her grandmothers hand cut wine glasses, and hopefully turn her exhausting trip into a elabrative night of love.

Her commission on this book was astronomical, and all she could think about were the possibilities now waiting for them. Her claim to fame was on the way. All the struggling would now be behind her and life was on the upswing.

The cab dropped her off at the front of the brownstone and she struggled to pull the suitcase up the long staircase.

"Oh for an apartment on the first floor" she mumbled to herself looking at all the stairs she was going to have to climb. "I think I will put that first on my agenda" she thought.

She stood in front of the door with the bottle of wine in one hand, suitcase next to her on the floor and keys in her other hand. She opened the door.

"Surprise Joe I am home early" she rang out. Joe standing naked in the living room was quite a sight. The naked girl on the couch however did not set very well.

"Ali, your home early" he coughed out the sweat now pouring down his ashen face.

"Not going to get out of this one easily are you Joe?" she replied staring at the naked boobs of the girl now scrambling to find her shirt and pants.

"Well, what a nice welcome home present. Oh don't leave sweetie" she said sarcastically as the girl scrambled to put on her clothes. Joe just stood there stark naked trying to explain.

"It's not what it seems" he fumbled for his words.

"Really, don't leave sweetie, stay with him, it seems you both deserve each other."

Ali was red with anger as she turned, grabbed her suitcase, and slammed the door behind her. How could he do that to her she thought and of all nights?

This was their one year anniversary. Another year wasted, down the drain. This time she was done with men.

“I am absolutely not the guilty one in this” she mumbled under her breath although in her head the guilt pushed through. Joe had tried many times to tell her he was lonely when she was gone, and she was gone a lot lately.

“Take a deep breath” she told herself softly as she hailed herself another cab.

She would stay at the hotel down the road until Eddie got her a rental car. She would just head off to New Haven early and spend a few days getting her head together before starting on the new tour. She was robotically handling the situation as usual. She had a need to put it into some neat little package to avoid the tears she was holding back. After all wasn’t this the normal thing for her to do compartmentalize things when chaos entered the scene.

“Call Eddie” she spoke to her cell phone again just as if nothing was wrong.

Move on, she internalized before the terror of it all would hit her from behind. The message machine came on so she started to leave him a message.

"Hey Eddie, do me a favor book me a hotel room tonight at the Historian, and if you haven't booked my trip do it now. I am going to leave first thing tomorrow and I will pick up a car at the rental place attached to the Historian. Thanks again Eddie, you're always my lifesaver."

"Hey, wait Ali, I am here. Hang on a minute."

She barely gave Eddie the chance to catch his breath as he stopped what he was doing and picked up the phone.

"What's up Ali? You sound upset."

Eddie could always tell when things were not going her way.

"It's ok Eddie just another jerk out of my life."

“Oh man, I can only imagine that it has to do with Joe and another woman?”

Eddie was very perceptive when it came to things of her heart. Eddie had been with her for several years now.

He had seen the guys come and go out of her life. Joe Dagger had lasted the longest.

He kept telling her that there was hope for her yet. What number was this, five, six? He wasn’t trying to keep track, but her record was pretty bad.

She hoped Eddie wasn’t counting but he probably was keeping close score. Maybe he was even betting on her, after all her love life was the joke of the office.

“Well Eddie, there was a naked woman in my apartment when I arrived home, and she was not exactly alone.” She said trying not to sob in the phone.

"Holy cow Ali, I am sorry about that one, but you know I told you he didn't seem like the type to wait around alone. If you want them to stay home you have to keep their tail a wagging."

"Where do you come up with this cheesy crap Eddie?"

"Authors Ali, where else"

"Well Eddie, you were right on the target with this one. What's wrong with me?

I can't seem to find someone that understands what writing means to me. All of this touring is just a part of it. Maybe I am better off alone."

"Nah, there is a guy out there somewhere who will understand you, and love you for who you are. It's hard being on that ladder going up. I think everyone falls for a few frogs before they find the right one." Eddie laughed.

He always had a way of turning things around and making her laugh.

“Well I wonder if Kermit is available” she asked Eddie joking about the frogs.

“I took care of all the reservations including the one here. Have a good trip and call me if you need something, even if it is just to talk.”

“Hey Eddie, just in case I am careless, thoughtless, and forgetful, thank you, you’re a great assistant and I definitely don’t tell you that enough.”

“Yeah, keep remembering that too. I will take care of everything for you. You just take care of yourself Ali. I’ll see you when you get back.”

She stumbled through the lobby tired, hurting, and dragging her heavy luggage behind her.

“God I have to learn to pack lighter.” She mumbled as she stopped at the front desk.

"I think I have a reservation?" she questionably told the attending clerk.

"Ali Watson is the name." She said as she wiped her hand across her face to get her straggly bangs out of her eyes.

"Ahhh yes, Ms. Watson, we do have you on for an overnight stay."

Thank God for Eddie, he comes through for me all the time she sighed as the busboy grabbed her suitcase.

"Follow me this way, please."

Before she got to her room there were fifteen calls from Joe.

"Baby, I'm sorry. You have to forgive me. Baby, it's just because I was lonely. You're gone all the time."

How tired she was of baby this, baby that. She was not going to call him. He was trying already to turn this all around making her the guilty one.

It would be as if she did this to him. All she wanted was a man to love her, appreciate what she does, and a warm body to come home to after a long book tour. Was that so much to ask for? Obviously it was according to Joe.

He was probably more worried about where he was going to stay if she decided to kick him out, then if she were coming back to him.

She would give him the apartment. After all it was hard to find one in New York and she didn't want to take anything that he and this woman's body fluids might be on. How gross she thought imagining the two of them naked on her couch.

After the tour she would pack her personal things and move out. She would have to find a place soon though.

It would be easier for her to relocate. She could write pretty much anywhere. His job was around the corner from the apartment, and she knew that he could handle the rent by himself.

It was a reasonable rate for the area and she had been lucky to find it when she did.

On this drive to New Haven she would take a look around and see what she could find in accommodations for herself. Maybe it was time that she grew up and faced the fact that she could only depend on herself. The phone rang again. She really hated confrontations, and this one with Joe was not something she was ready to verbally address just yet.

She didn't answer but she did text him that she would be moving out, and he could keep the apartment end of conversation.

He left her a few more cell phone messages to call and discuss, but she was not ready for the sweet talk that he was known for.

The naked bodies embraced on her couch were still too fresh in her mind.

All she wanted was her bottle of wine, and a good night's sleep now. She crawled on the bed opened the bottle of wine and took a slug. This was not what she had pictured she would be doing on her anniversary, sucking up a bottle of wine, all by herself in a hotel room. She finally munched the chocolates on the pillow and fell asleep with wine bottle in hand.

The next morning she woke with a major headache. She pulled herself out of the bed and headed toward the shower. A nice hot shower would surely help the pounding to stop.

She gathered her few items and checked out of the hotel. The desk clerk had her checked out in record time with the car ordered by Eddie waiting out front.

"The rental car is waiting for you out front Ms. Watson" she said with the flair of an aspiring actress.

It seemed that in New York most young women her age in these kinds of jobs were aspiring actresses waiting for their big break.

She loved the dramatics they would present to each customer hoping to be discovered by some lingering major producer- director. You never knew who they were unless they had an entourage of starlets around them

"May I take you to your car? May I give you your receipt?" All very dramatically performed a little overkill she thought.

"Eddie is greatest, I have to remember to give him a raise" she said as she left him a message about the new red mustang sitting out front just waiting for her to get into the driver's seat.

The car was a spark of delight, a gem, and hopefully no speeding ticket looming in her future as she took off heading for the thruway.

Everyone in New York was a speeder, but she was behind the wheel of a sparkling red mustang and speeding was required of this vehicle.

Zero to sixty in nothing flat.

That is just what she needed a hot car and a cool drink. I will save the drinks for later once I get to New Haven she thought. Chill out at the bar, have a good time and forget about the cheating ex-boyfriend. Speeding down the highway with the radio blasting…singing "Hey Bartender, give me another shot of crown."

Chapter Two

Ali had been speeding along the old country road not paying much attention to what was ahead of her when suddenly something sprinted out in front of her car. She slammed on the brakes but the ice covered road was slippery enough to send the car into a tail spin. Her car spun off the main road, into a deep snow bank, finally ending up with the front end in a ditch. She sat with her hands clenched to the steering wheel trying to catch her breath.

"I'm ok, I'm ok" she mumbled to herself.

She was now wondering why she decided to drive instead of fly to New Haven. The snow was falling lightly for the moment but the roads had quickly turned into pure sheets of ice. She shifted the car into reverse, but the wheels just kept spinning.

"Great this is just what I need. Stuck in this ditch on a deserted road and I haven't seen another car in at least a half hour."

She tried to inch forward, but each time it just sent the wheels into a spinning frenzy. She had to face the fact she was stranded in a ditch, her cell phone in dead zone, with nothing but snow covered roads surrounding her.

What a way to end up, frozen to death, buried under a ton of snow, behind the wheel of a sports car, on an old country road. It sounded like a scene from one of her mystery books.

Venturing out into the snow did not seemed like a better scenario, but maybe there was a house nearby where she could get help. At least she would be moving and feeling like she might be accomplishing something instead of just sitting in the cold dying alone.

Just maybe a car would come by and rescue her. Yeah, that was wishful thinking. She pulled out her hat and gloves and bundled up before exiting the car.

She climbed up the snow bank cursing while she slid down twice before being able to get her footing.

She tried to dig the car out but that was just a waste of time and now she was really cold.

If she walked a ways just maybe there was a house nearby. A flash of light caught her eye. It looked as though it came from the end of the snow covered road. She thought that maybe she was somewhere near the ocean. The biting winds were cutting through her coat like a knife. Maybe it was a lighthouse flashing a warning out to sea, or a reflection from some kind of glass.

She kept walking there was no going back now. It was hard to tell where the light came from. The closer she got to the ocean the harder the wind and snow blew against her, blinding her sight.

"What is that?" she asked herself struggling to see.

"Something is ahead." She whispered to herself moving as quickly as she could in the biting cold. Her hands and face were frozen and she felt the ice crystals sticking to her eyelashes.

She struggled against the harsh winds as she tried to follow the light pulling her coat closer around her as the winds tore through the material. As she got closer to the reflection she was able to see the cliff ahead. The waves were crashing against the rocks and the spray of water turned quickly into ice droplets settling to the ground.

There against the backdrop of the cliff, was her salvation in the storm. A huge Victorian home hidden from the rest of the world.

"I hope that someone lives here" she said to herself silently.

It had to be better to be inside this old house then sitting in the car asphyxiating herself from the exhaust until her gas ran out.

The old house loomed tall and eerie looking. In fact she imagined someone like Edgar Allen Poe living in an estate such as this.

The structural features and hand carved shutters and doors were large and overbearing and yet, it had a sense of lingering elegance in its presentation. The tower loomed above the house with a rod iron rail porch surrounding it. The vicious waves in violent anger seemed to splash against the wrought iron rails turning them into ice statues that seemed to be standing watch from the tower.

Her writers mind wandered off in thought, or maybe she was just hallucinating from the cold. She wondered if the owner was a seafarer. Possibly his loving wife walked the tower rail looking for his ship to arrive, while the lighthouse shined its light to save his ship from the rocks below.

The lighthouse off in the distance was perfectly placed on a small rock island in the cove just past the cliff. Watching its light circle around and around made it a perfect scene.

As prestigious and elegant as this home might once have been it now looked as though it had been neglected for many years. She was stranded and this was a sanctuary in the blizzard that had swept its way in so quickly. She could hope that there might be someone in the house who would able to assist her in getting help. Then yet again, she feared that there might be someone in the house that could keep her from getting help. She had to take the chance. She could no longer feel her feet.

There was a worn out sign on the gate. The sign could have been saying the house was for sale or rent, but the letters were worn off she had no way of knowing. She could only hope it wasn't one of those beware of the guard dog signs.

As she opened the gate a strong cold wind whipped it from her hand, and she fought against it trying to keep her balance. She had to get inside. She didn't want someone to find her frozen body buried in snow and ice come spring.

The front stairs creaked from the cold as she moved up them carefully trying not to slip.

The stained glass window in the front door was exquisite even though it obviously had not been cleaned in years, and visibility of the inside of the house was nonexistent as she tried to peer through the dirt and grime.

The main windows were blocked by thick maroon and gold color drapes making it impossible to see if anyone actually lived there. She knocked several times but no one answered, so she tried the door. Surprisingly it opened creaking almost as badly as the stairs.

She called inside but it was obvious by the cobwebs hanging from the crystal chandelier that no one had lived in the home in quite some time. The furniture was covered with dingy white sheets all of them covered in dust. Dirty ghosts of the past haunting the living room she thought.

The old oak floors which she assumed at one time had been beautiful were now covered with scratch's, dirt, and old leaves. She slowly walked into what was at one time an elegant entry parlor. The musty smell told her it had been a while since anyone had resided in this magnificent home.

She closed her eyes as she entered the living room trying to imagine what it might have been like to live in a home such as this at the turn of the century. Her imagination took her on a wild adventure as she pictured herself in a long frilly gown with sequins around the bodice.

She could hear the music of a small violin and viola quartet playing the Venetian waltz softly in the background as dignitaries and businessmen mingling amongst themselves.

She was so hungry now that she could envision the food spread out on a banquet table fit for a king.

The servants handing drinks to the men who were standing, talking of their newest conquests and the treasures they brought back with them on their ships.

This vision was so real in her head that she turned to face the sound of a man's voice standing before the fireplace. She took a deep breath in. Yes, it was a sweet cherry tobacco just like she remembered as a child. Her grandpa would light up as he sat in his chair. She would curl up next to him taking in the smell, making a memory in her head while grandma complained that his stinky pipe would be the death of her.

There he was a handsome swashbuckler, of a man. A true sailor tanned from the sun that caressed his skin as he stood on the deck of the ship. He was the Captain, smiling, laughing, and telling tall tales of the sea while his eyes went about searching the room.

He was looking for someone; his deep blue eyes drew her in until he reached out to take her hand in his.

The fire behind him sent out warmth that rippled through her body. Suddenly the cold draft from the open door brought her back to reality. She opened her eyes just as the door slammed shut. Her heart skipped a beat. Where was she? Oh yes, warmth was what she needed right now as she stood shivering in the cold damp room. She could start a fire all she needed was some wood and a lighter. She fumbled through her purse looking for her lighter.

"Oh there you are." she sighed a sense of relief. How lucky could she be there was wood already stacked in the fireplace as if someone were expecting her?

The old stone fireplace with the cedar mantle was breathtaking. Architecture of this kind was rarely found anymore. She glanced above the fireplace trying to warm her hands on the small fire that she had managed to start.

"Oh my God" she let out a cry of bewilderment as she gazed at the portrait above the mantle.

There above the mantle hung a portrait of her swashbuckling Captain. He was elegantly dressed sitting in an old leather chair with pipe in hand. Typical of the early 1900's there was no expression on his face. He had brown wavy hair but most remarking were his eyes. They were the deepest blue, almost as blue as the ocean water. In fact only her mother's eyes could compare with that shade of blue she thought.

The eeriness of the portrait was that his eyes almost seemed to follow her movements. She had allowed her imagination to far surpass itself this time.

After all here she was in this house uninvited and truthfully afraid that someone might just catch her trespassing. Even though the fire was warming her it seemed as though something in the room made her shiver.

She toyed with the idea that a little hard work this house could be restored to its previous beauty.

The privacy of it being the only house on a dead end street would be perfect for her concentration. She wondered who owned it and if maybe they would be willing to sell. Thoughts were pouring into her brain as if someone had opened the Watergates and she was swept up in the rush. She could see herself writing a story about the man in the painting. He had to be a ship's captain or a nobleman.

The story was already building in her head. This whole thing was just perfect for her next novel. She wiped the frame of the painting where a metal plate was engraved. Captain Masterson B. Ravenswood, now that name sounded masterful.

"Captain Ravenswood." She sounded off the name as if she were presenting herself to him making a little curtsy before the painting. There must be some history, a story, to go along with this painting she thought as she jotted the name down in the writing journal she always carried in her pocket.

What an intriguing story this would make. She was already titling the book in her head.

The Captain and his Lady she thought as a workable title. That is if he had a lady. Of course he had to have a lady he was much too handsome to be alone especially in this huge house. He had to have a family.

She wandered through the house as if each room were calling out her name. The music room had a beautiful grand piano with an old cherry stain finish on it. She touched a few keys; it was badly out of tune but it most certainly had been a beautiful instrument in its day.

She pulled the white sheets from the dining room table and chairs. The furniture was elegant and the table and chairs looked as if they were hand carved wood. The chairs stood tall and strong made of the finest oak.

There were intricately carved roses at the top of each chair and she wondered who the craftsman was.

Hungry she ventures into the kitchen hoping that there might be some scrap of something to eat. The kitchen was large and roomy with a wood slab table set up in the middle of it for the servants to utilize. There was a large pantry off the kitchen that still had some empty old canning jars neatly sitting on the shelves as if they were patiently waiting to be filled.

Inside the pantry was a small door that creaked loudly as she opened it. A secret staircase hidden in the pantry, how mysterious was that? Who could ever resist investigating where it went? Not her that is for sure. She followed the narrow staircase that ended at the second floor. At the top of the stairs there was another door leading into a very small room. The room was very plain and cobwebs hung everywhere from the ceiling.

The only furniture in this small room was a single bed and a small antique dresser with a circular mirror. It was blackened and decayed with time and she could barely see her reflection in it. Oddly enough there was a smell of lavender, no lilac maybe? It seemed to permeate the room.

Strange how that smells of perfume could have lingered in this room over the years. It was strong though and very prominent when she opened the dresser drawer. The small room had two more doors, one leading to the main hallway, and the other to a large bedroom she assumed was at one time a nursery.

The nursery walls were painted a blue gray color so she figured that it must have been a boy's room. The small wooden crib looked hand carved and the lacquer was peeling off from age. There was something about the room that seemed not quite right, a feeling, but she couldn't figure it out. It was almost as if there was a lingering sadness in the air.

She wondered if the Captain and his wife had a son. The woman who cared for him must have stayed in the small room above the pantry. What a story this could become she thought as she wandered further through the house.

Curiosity now had Ali captured in its spell; she needed to know who owned this home, and why it had been left in such disrepair. It had so much potential it was hard to believe that no one took any interest in renovating it.

She walked the hallway peering into each room. The old wallpaper on the walls was pealing and yet it had an air of elegance. The master bedroom was at the end of the hall surprisingly the farthest room from the nursery. It was larger than the rest of the rooms. It had a huge canopy bed with a down filled mattress. In its day it had to be an expensive extravagance not to mention its worth now as an antique. The oak frame was carved similar to the dining room chairs, only this had a quaint little village in the center surrounded by the same types of roses. The dressers in the room matched it perfectly.

There was a fireplace with another painting over it. This one was of a beautiful woman. Her long blonde hair hung down her back with several strands braided in a crown around her head. It was quite stoic, no smile on her face, no emotion to be seen.

Quite the prim and proper lady of the house Ali assumed. She wiped the metal plate on this painting to find the name Mistress Mary Alice Wentworth Ravenswood. This must certainly be the Mistress of the house, wife of the Captain perhaps? This room seemed to be screaming out its own story.

Ali could never walk away from a good story, and she had a feeling that this one was going to be a great one. She jotted down Wentworth and headed back down the beautiful winding staircase that led back to the entryway. This house was so inviting. It made her feel as if she belonged there.

She could not believe that it had been abandoned like this. She was going to do some investigative work and find out who owned this home. Even as a child writing the story had always been her passion. Renovating this house would be like uncovering a deep dark secret. Wasn't that what writing was all about? Discovering the secrets as the story unfolds itself.

She was definitely going to have to find out who owned it, and if there was any way that she could come in and fix this into a livable home again. Just as she reached for the front door a swift breeze passed her face leaving her with a chill.

"A little drafty in here I guess" she spoke out loud to calm the queasy feeling in her stomach.

She reached for the glass knob on the door once more and tried to turn it. It was almost as though someone was holding it from the outside it would not budge.

She yanked on it hard until finally the door gave way and she ended up propelled across the room with her butt promptly on the floor.

Now that was strange she thought to herself. It was almost as if the house didn't want her to leave. She turned to reclose the door when suddenly her phone beeped out a message. She had cell service? How strange that before she seemed to be in a dead zone. Eddie had texted her.

It was the name of the Inn he had set her up in. According to her GPS it was about ten miles down the main road. The snow had come down hard and she could barely even see the red of her car down the road. There was no way that she was leaving anytime soon.

Nervous about the status of her phone, and afraid she might lose service once more she promptly called for help. Luckily it was a small town and the tow truck was readily available. It took him over an hour to get there and he had to call a snow plow to plow her out, but eventually her rental was out of the ditch and she was on back on the road.

She had gathered all the information she needed the address, the street, and decided she would make a special stop at the county court house before heading to the Inn. Her investigative brain was in overdrive and she wasn't going to stop until she scrounged up the name of the owner. She carefully pulled out onto the main road and headed out to the center of town.

Dan was very precise in giving her directions and his card should she get stuck in any ditches or large piles of snow. He made a joke that he was at her beck and call and then winked at her. It had been quite a day; she was tired and looking forward to finding some place where she could quietly enjoy a nice hot meal and a drink or two.

Dan had mentioned that the Lighthouse Bar and Grill was a nice place to eat so she might just have to check it out while she was in town.

As she pulled into the small town of Ravensport she noticed how backwards the town seemed to be. All of the street lights were old fashioned gas-powered lights. In fact it looked as if she had gone back a century in time. How quaint she thought seeing the gazebo in the center of the village and a small ice-skating rink set up just on the other side. The children were laughing and skating, building ice forts and snowmen.

It was somehow unusual to see kids outside running and playing in the snow. Where she came from children were mostly bundled up in blankets or snugglies parked in front of some TV or video game.

The Ravensport Courthouse was attached to the Ravensport Library situated at the center of the town. The old clock tower in the building chimed four times as she pulled in and parked the car. She tried to walk carefully up the courthouse stairs, but she kept slipping on the ice. Inside she was promptly met by an elderly lady her hair tied up in a bun behind her head.

She looked like the chief librarian from some old movie. She introduced herself to Ali as Lindy Westbetter while shushing some of the children who were reading out loud. It was apparent that she was in charge of both the county records and the library. She was wearing a pinstriped suit with what Ali considered to be basic black old lady shoes. The same kind her great grandma used to wear.

She was very young but she remembered the old lady shoes, the smell of her sweet lilac perfume, and the beautiful heart-shaped locket that she wore around her neck. She never went anywhere without that locket around her neck.

"Oh there are many stories about that house my dear. Some say it is haunted, some say it is cursed. No one with any sense has ever inquired about renting or buying it that I am aware of. Truthfully I wasn't sure that anyone has lived in the house since Mistress Mary Ravenswood left with her son Matthew back in the early 1900's."

She paused as she opened the book, scanning down through the records to see if she could find the current owner.

"The old Ravenswood mansion has been empty many years now. It is written here that a relative did move in with her two boys for a short time probably ten or fifteen years ago though. One of the boys is listed as the owner. Here is the information you are requesting.

I wasn't sure that I would be able to locate who currently owns it. It seems that Mr. Beauregard Ravenswood a great grandson of Captain Ravenswood actually still holds the title to Ravenswood Manor. I must admit I am a bit surprised that he still owns it."

Ravenswood Manor, what a perfect name for the Victorian mansion she thought.

"Why do you say that?" Ali asked since it seemed a strange kind of statement to make.

"Why wouldn't family still own the house?"

The house has quite a shady past to it. If you leave me your cell phone number I will see if I can get a hold of Mr. Ravenswood's current phone number for you."

Now Ali was really intrigued by the mystery surrounding Ravenswood Manor. She thanked Miss Westbetter and asked her how she could gather any more information regarding the mansion and its history.

"Well, truthfully Ms. Watson, Pearl Carter at the Ravensport Inn is the best person to ask. She claims to know the whole truth about Ravenswood Manor and its occupants. You can't believe everything she says though she is very old and a little crazy at times. Her niece Jessica runs the Inn, Pearl would be the best person to talk to if your desire is some history on that old place. Pearl claims that her grandmother was the cook for the Captain and his wife. So if anyone knows the stories or tall tales if you ask me, well she would certainly know them all. After all I know nothing about those tall tales."

"Well thank you Mrs. Westbetter for all that information. I will definitely seek out Mrs. Carter."

Mrs. Westbetter turned and headed back to her desk muttering under her breath.

"The old captain is doing it again. She mumbled." I try my hardest to discourage them but they just keep coming in here asking too many questions. This one seems a little different though. The captain must have something else in mind this time. I don't know why he just doesn't give up. If he doesn't stop soon people will think everyone in this town is crazy. "

How lucky could she get? It was like Eddie had some mystical power knowing exactly where she needed to stay.

This was the very Inn that he called and made reservations for; of course it wasn't until later that Ali found out it was also the only Inn in the town of Ravensport.

She walked into the front lobby of the Ravensport Inn and found it to be more like an old boarding house than an Inn but quite a friendly place.

“Welcome to our Inn” the young girl said as she walked up to the counter. “How can I assist you?”

Her short brown hair curled around her face in little ringlets reminding Maddie of a picture of someone who had their hair done in pin curls back in the 1930’s and 40’s. She almost looked like one of those cute little flapper girls all she was missing was the fringed dress.

“Hi I am Ali Watson; I believe my assistant booked me a room here at your Inn.”

“Oh yes, we have been expecting you. Welcome Ms. Watson; it is a privilege for us that you decided to choose our little inn for your stay. Most of the writers that come through here head on up to the big city hotels so we are really happy that you decided to stay with us.”

“Why thank you, but I believe you owe it all to Eddie my assistant.

He is the one who chooses where I stay and I have always counted on his good taste to put me up in the best. Your Inn looks like the perfect place to write. Tell me..." she paused.

"Oh its Jessica I'm sorry I meant to introduce myself."

"Jessica, wonderful then, where might I find a Mrs. Pearl Carter?"

Jessica looked puzzled why in the world would this stranger ask to see her crazy Aunt Pearl?

"Do you know my Aunt?" she questioned.

"Oh I don't know her, but Ms. Westbetter at the Library told me that your Aunt might be able to fill me in on some local history. I am interested in the story behind the Ravenswood Manor."

Jessica took a deep breath, her face went white.

"Are you sure you want to know about the Manor?" she acted as if no one dare breathe a word about the Manor.

"Yes, I do want to know about it. In fact I am hoping that I will be able to rent or buy the place from the owner."

"You're kidding right?" Jessica asked thinking that this city girl is crazy to want to buy Ravenswood Manor.

"No Jessica, however you are making me very curious with your reaction to my question."

"Well I will let Aunt Pearl tell you its history, she is the most knowledgeable, but don't count on it being extremely accurate her memory is fading. My Aunt is quite elderly you see, and I think sometimes her imagination takes over where the truth ends. You will find her sitting in her rocking chair in the sun room at the back of the Inn. I will take your luggage to your room. I gave you the one at the back of the house. It is quieter there and you're less likely to be disturbed."

"Thank you Jessica" she replied as she headed to find this mysterious Aunt Pearl.

Chapter Three

She was sitting almost seemingly pacing herself as she rocked back and forth with her back to Ali.

"What is your name my dear?" she asked as Ali walked through the door.

"He told me you would come asking questions." She said as if she was expecting her the whole time.

"Who told you?" Ali asked.

"The captain, of course, who else" she responded.

"The captain" Ali replied now understanding what Jessica was alluding to as she moved to face Aunt Pearl.

"Yes, Captain Ravenswood. He said you are still as beautiful as he remembers, so I have to assume you are someone special to him."

"You talk to Captain Ravenswood? "She asked again.

"Didn't I just say that my dear."

"Well my name Alexandria Elizabeth Watson to answer your first question but everyone calls me Ali."

"Maybe I am wrong my dear, but I could swear he called you Lizzie.

"No, my name is Ali; I was named after my great grandmother who was nicknamed Lizzie."

"Yes, oh my yes, the captain is thinking of Lizzie O'Malley of course" she rattled off as if she were remembering an old friend from the past. "You must resemble her quite a bit since he is so adamant about seeing his Lizzie."

"My great grandmother was Alexandria Elizabeth McPherson" she replied.

"Of course my dear, he is just mistaken that's all. The Captain I mean. Of course you are not his Lizzie. You couldn't possibly be his Lizzie. She is long dead."

Aunt Pearl smiled but kept silent about the last name.

"It is very interesting my dear, the fact that you resemble the Captain's Miss Lizzie so much." She replied. "Maybe that is why he seems so attracted to you."

"I see you found Aunt Pearl." Jessica stated as she brought in some hot tea and cookies on a platter.

"I was sure that you both could use some refreshments while you talk."

"Thank you my dear, it is as if you read my mind. Please help yourself."

Aunt Pearl had some strange ways about her. Ali estimated she was in her late eighties and very eccentric. She was blind, although Ali thought that maybe she had a little vision left. Aunt Pearl's hair was gray and curly, and she reminded her a little of a shriveled up poodle.

There was one thing she was sure of and that was that Jessica was very protective of her Aunt.

It was as if she screened everyone very closely who inquired of her Aunt's somewhat strange talents. Ali chuckled as she talked with Pearl. She was quite the character and Ali was sure that Pearl could truly convince anyone that the Captain conversed with her most every day.

Ali sat for several hours with Aunt Pearl. She wanted to gather as much information as she could from this woman who seemed to have an acute knowledge of everything that happened in Ravenswood.

"They say that wisdom is wasted on the old people, but I tell my niece Jessica that it is wasted on the young. The young pay no mind to the important things that is why they miss out on all the adventure life has in store."

Aunt Pearl started out each of her conversations with what was laughingly referred to as her pearls of wisdom.

Out of nowhere Ali noticed a soft chill in the air and then a sweet smell of roses wafted around her and Miss Pearl as she sat rocking in her chair.

"Is there a rose garden close by here?" Ali asked.

"Why hello Miss Mary, and how are you today?" Ali turned to see if anyone had entered the room, but there was no one.

"Oh Miss Mary, what frets you so? This young lady is just inquiring about you and the Captain that's all. I don't know Miss Mary; our conversation hasn't gone that far yet."

"Ali, Miss Mary is inquiring of why you're so interested in her family? She seems upset that you're seeking out all this information."

"I am just curious about the history of Ravensport that is all Miss Pearl."

She stammered trying to figure out what exactly was happening here. Ali felt a rush of cold move past her with another smell of Roses.

"Where is that smell of roses coming from?" Ali asked.

"Oh that's Miss Mary; she just loves that rose perfume. Sometimes she wears it much too strong. Miss Lizzie on the other hand well she loved sweet lilac; if you smell a soft scent of lilac then Miss Lizzie is probably somewhere close by."

"What about the Captain? Does he have a smell too?" she added to get over the awkwardness of this conversation.

"Oh yes, his is of Cherry tobacco He is always smoking his pipe and cherry tobacco is his favorite. You think I am crazy don't you Ali?" She laughed.

"I am not sure what to think." She replied pausing for a moment to gain some courage.

“I have never met anyone who believes that they talk with dead people before.”

“You have to be open my dear, if you don’t believe than you can’t see them. They are here with us right now, except for Miss Lizzie of course. When she comes, and it is not very often she always comes alone, and never when Mary or the Captain is present.”

“The captain is quite intrigued with you. He believes that you are his Lizzie. You must resemble her quite a bit for him to think that. He has been searching years for her. For some reason their spirits cannot seem to find each other. I haven’t figured out why.”

“I don’t understand why would he think I am this Lizzie?”

“Well, he says that you were led back to the house so that his prayers would be answered.”

“What prayer?”

“For many years it has been his prayer that God would allow him to see and speak to Lizzie one last time. To let him explain, resolve his issue with her.”

“How and why would he think that I could be her?”

“I am afraid that you must resemble her very much. Let me tell you his story.”

“You see the captain was a handsome young man. His parents were very wealthy and they owned the Shipping business in Ravensport. Oh Miss Ali, to be totally honest they really owned the entire town.”

“The Ravenswood’s hired a young couple straight from Ireland who had a little girl around the same age as the Captain. They played together their whole lives. They fell in love but she was not of the same status as the Ravenswood’s and so as they grew into adulthood they were forbidden to associate. Lizzie’s father took ill and passed away and her mother soon suffered the same fate.

Lizzy was alone she knew of no other family then the Ravenswood's. Mary took pity on her and gave her the job of chamber maid. Pity wasn't really Mary's strong suit. She basically told Lizzie that her parents owed them a huge debt, and she would have to work it off in this manner, or be sent to the poor house. Trust me that no one deserved to live in what they sadly called the poor house. It was a sad den of iniquity where most of the women ended up being sex slaves just to survive."

"What happened after that, I mean, obviously this Miss Lizzie stayed, but what happened between her and the Captain? I would love to hear this whole story, can you tell it to me?"

"Wouldn't you rather hear it from the Captain himself? I might relay it incorrectly."

"Aunt Pearl, I don't think that is possible for him to tell the story. He isn't alive any longer."

"Death has never stopped him before my dear."

She started rocking in her chair gazing out into the garden that was currently covered in snow. Her silence was deafening.

"He says my dear, he will reveal what you need to know, but you need to rest first. His soul has been very weak lately. Now that you have arrived, he will regain his strength and when the time is right he will tell you all that has transpired in the years of separation."

Chills went up Ali's spine as she once again felt that cold breeze pass by her face. It was extremely familiar like the one she felt at Ravenswood Manor. She closed her eyes and took in a deep breath. Cherry pipe smoke permeated her nose.

"He has left my dear, he does wish for you to rest. It has been a long day."

"Are you ready for bed Aunt Pearl" Jessica came in, almost as if she had been summoned.

"Yes my dear, I am quite tired. Many visitors today you know. They tire me out. I will see you tomorrow Ali?" she asked.

"Yes, I believe so." She replied. "I think a good night's sleep will clear my head."

What she really wanted to do was write all this down in her journal in hopes that she wouldn't forget any of the details.

Jessica had placed her bags in a room at the back of the Inn. She told her that this room was the quietest room in the Inn. She should be able to sleep soundly as if all this talk about the Captain would allow her to sleep at all. Her experience with Aunt Pearl had been exhilarating and although she was tired, she was sure her mind would be rambling all night.

The room was quite warm so she opened the window slightly to bring in a slight breeze. A strong odor of cherry tobacco came rushing into the room.

The smell was almost intoxicating and yet it seemed to make her drowsier by the moment. She closed the window and sat on the bed. Aunt Pearl was definitely a strange character. She couldn't possibly believe that she speaks with the Captain. She was just an old woman with tales to tell and she just believed she spoke to the Captain and his wife because she was lonely.

She glanced at the night stand and noticed the light flashing on her cell phone. She had missed a call. She pressed the voicemail and there was a message from Miss Westbetter. She had left a phone number for Mr. Ravenswood that she had located. It was late so Ali decided she would wait until tomorrow to make the call.

She lay back on the bed trying hard to fall asleep but her mind was sorting through all the strange events of the day. Where was that smell coming from? It seemed to swirl around her.

"I am just tired and imagining things" she mumbled as she fell into a deep sleep.

He sat on the edge of the bed, watching her intently. The aura of his presence glowed in the moonlight. She was beautiful, his Lizzie, just as he remembered her. Her brown hair curled around her face in ringlets. Her lips so inviting he could not stop himself as he gently kissed her.

"Lizzie you have finally returned to me." He sighed again. "I knew it was you the moment you walked through the door. The smell of lilacs will fill the house once more. Very soon we will be together again my love."

He stroked her face with his hand wanting her to respond to his touch, yet knowing she could not feel, hear, or see him. She would feel his presence soon. He was gaining strength from her essence. Soon he would be strong enough and she would know that he was there. He had returned from his voyage and he needed to know why she had not been waiting for him. Soon he would have his answer. He would know why she had left.

Chapter Four

Early the next morning Ali called the number that was left on her cell phone. "This is Beau, please leave me your message and I will get back to you as soon as possible."

She stuttered not knowing exactly what to say.

"Hi, this is Ali Watson and I am interested in renting, or buying the house that you own on Ravenswood Cliff. Can you call me back at this number and let me know if it is possible to meet and discuss this possible transaction?"

Ali hung up the phone and headed downstairs to the family room where Jessica told her breakfast would be served family style. She walked down the hallway and headed toward the smell of bacon that permeated the hallways.

Several people were already at the table eating. It did look like a big family function everyone gathered together at the long table in the dining room.

She was used to eating alone but enjoyed the fellowship that seemed to be going on with Miss Pearl sitting at the head of the table.

"Welcome Miss Ali" Pearl greeted her as she walked into the room. She still couldn't figure out how she could tell who was walking into the room, yet she seemed to know everyone by name.

Please meet Mr. and Mrs. Duncan from Vermont, and the Carvers are here from California. Everyone let me introduce Ms. Alexandria Watson the famous New York author. Ali wished she hadn't done that she was trying hard to remain anonymous. Everyone there just nodded their head and continued to eat. It was fairly obvious that none of them were avid book readers or they would have recognized her name.

The food was fabulous. Jessica had set up a fruit bar along with pancakes, waffles, hot cereal and yogurt.

Some of the best hotels she had stayed in didn't offer anything like this smorgasbord of food.

After the meal she headed back to her room. "It must be a dead zone thing in this town." She mumbled trying to figure out how she had missed another call.

"Crap, it was from Mr. Ravenswood too."

The message was cordial. I am Beau Ravenswood and I am delighted that you are interested in Ravenswood Manor. I would much like to meet and show you the house. Please call me back and we can set up a time for that meeting.

.....

Beau was pleased that he had another interested party in the house. He wanted to dump it on some unsuspecting buyer for an outrageous price. It had been nothing but trouble for him since he inherited it.

He had tried to sell it several times before but for some strange reason, right before the sales went through the buyers always backed out.

They said it just didn't feel right, or the place was haunted. He could understand that though.

Every time he walked into that house he would feel an icy chill go down his back. He just figured it was the bad heating system. It was big and being so old it had a lot of drafty areas. It just needed insulation and a better furnace he told himself.

One thing for sure the house needed an upgrade on its heating system. The old wood fireplaces were not going to make it in today's market. He just didn't want to invest any more money into the old monster.

.....

Ali was excited by the call. She dialed the number back. The phone rang and rang.

"Please pick up" she whispered to herself.

"Hi"

The sound of his voice answering was music to her ears.

"Hi," she returned the greeting. "I am Ali Watson, the person interested in your home on Ravenswood Cliff."

"Yes, wonderful, I was hoping that you would call back. I would love to set up a time for us to go to the house and I can tell you some of its history. Then if you're still interested we can discuss a price and start the process."

He wanted to hit himself, he was way too anxious to sell. He hoped she didn't pick up on that. It would lower the price right off the bat if she thought he was trying to dump the place.

"Personally, Outside of a couple times to show other buyers I haven't been to the house in a long time."

"I am sure it is going to be quite dirty and dusty. I hope that you take that into consideration when you look at the place. My great grandmother and grandfather, and so on down the line used to live in it. Maybe you heard about Captain Masterson and Mary Ravenswood?"

"I have heard a couple stories about the Captain, but I would love to hear about the history behind the house. I am a writer and I am always up for a good story."

"You would love this one then." He laughed.

The sound of his laugh was captivating.

"Then let's do it. How about we meet at the house tomorrow around noon?"

"Sounds great Ms. Watson, I will meet you there."

Again the smell of roses surrounded her and she felt a cold chill go down her back as she hung up the phone.

This boarding house or Inn whatever they called it had some drafty rooms.

She shook off the feeling and grabbed her coat and purse. She had a meeting to talk with the bookstore owner today about the beginning of her book tour and she couldn't afford to be late. Her book Wintery Seduction was going to be one of her better books and she wanted to get the marketing of it out there as soon as possible. If she was going to buy Ravenswood Manor she would need all the money she could get her hands on.

……

She pulled up to the manor and just as before she was drawn to its hidden beauty. This time she would hear the stories behind the pictures on the walls. She would gain insight as to why this house seemed to call out to her.

"Hi, you must be Ali" he spoke as he opened her car door for her. What a gentleman she thought. Joe never opened anything for her except maybe a beer bottle.

"It's a pleasure to meet you Mr. Ravenswood."

"Call me Beau, please I hate being so formal."

"Well then Beau, call me Ali, and it is a pleasure to meet you."

He was tall and his blonde hair was cut in a stylish fashion. His deep brown eyes were like melted chocolate and his lips, well they were strawberry red. Any girl in her right mind would be happy to devour him, but she wasn't looking for any male companionship. At least that is what she kept telling herself.

"Keep your mind on business Ali" she whispered to herself.

He wore a dark navy suit probably an Armani, with a royal blue tie. He was definitely a wealthy man. With his looks he was probably more playboy type than business type. She could only hope that he was willing to let the house go for a reasonable price that she could afford. If his clothes said anything at all she would never be able to afford this.

"I am hoping you're ready for this because the house I am sure is in disarray. I personally have not been here in several years."

She didn't know if she should tell him that she had already been in the house. It had been her salvation that day. No, she should probably keep that to herself.

She reached for the handle but the door was locked. How strange she thought. It wasn't locked the other day.

He went to the door and brought out his keys.

"One of these things unlocks the door" he chuckled.

She stood there watching him fumble through key after key until he finally found the right one.

"These old houses have their idiosyncrasies you know. Hopefully the door isn't stuck shut."

He pulled on it a few times and finally it swung open. "Guess we have to fix that." He chuckled.

"As I have said before, I haven't really been here in a long time. I usually have the real estate woman show the house. For some reason this time I thought it best that I show you around personally."

"Well, that is very nice of you. I like the personal touch." She smiled.

"Where would you like to start? The upstairs or this floor first?"

"Let's start with the living room"

She took a deep breath as she entered the room.

"Is that your great grandfather?" she asked pointing to the portrait above the fireplace.

"Yes, that is Captain Ravenswood. They say he was a scoundrel, loved the women and had one in every port.

My grandmother used to tell me what a conniver he was, or maybe she used the word scalawag, and how I should never take after him. I don't know he looks pretty respectable in the portrait don't you think?"

"I can see he is quite handsome, so I can assume that women probably threw themselves at him."

Beau laughed at her statement. "Well he had some charm at least that is what I was told. Hopefully, I have inherited some of it."

"I never met him. Well I can't say that is true I was just too young to remember him.

He was lost at sea so my grandmother said. She called him a rogue and a womanizer totally uncouth. You see my great grandmother came from a wealthy family. The Wentworth's were well known in the importing business. Being from a seafaring family her father wanted Captain Ravenswood to bring back the spoils of his travels to enhance their wealth.

He and the Captains father felt the only way to combine wealth and resources were to force their children into marriage.

The Ravenswood's had been one of the founding families of Ravensport hence the name of the town. To have their son marry into the Wentworth fortune, well that was a dream come true. Together the two families would own the shipping business and the town.

My great grandfather started out as a cabin boy on the ship of pirate Captain John Moreland.

Moreland taught him all the tricks to the trade, and eventually my great grandfather took over the ship at the death of Captain Moreland.

The story goes that the marital joining of the Captain, and my great grandmother Mary, was the business deal of the century. This meant that everything that the Captain brought in would become Wentworth property. The Wentworth's made a fortune off of him.

He got honor and prestige in exchange. The story has changed over the years I am sure. No one will ever know the real truth I think.

These are just the ramblings of my mother, grandmother and great grandmother. Of course the story would be told in their favor and not the Captains."

"Well maybe that is why in the portrait he has no smile. That bargain couldn't have been very conducive to falling in love. Maybe that is why your grandmother and great grandmother called him a rogue."

"According to my mother, great grandma Mary was quite a looker. She had men who would do anything to be with her.

As much as she claimed my great grandfather as being the rogue I believe that she was quite a rogue herself. I don't remember her but the stories well, they remain. It wasn't until a few years ago that I returned here.

My mother passed away a few years ago and for some strange reason she left this house to me and my brother in her will. We were told that my great grandfather the Captain died at sea.

When he didn't return my great grandmother left with a man named Wilson Bradley and they moved to Maine. My grandmother said that was the last time that the family heard of her until some lawyer notified them of her death. The house was passed down through the family ending with me and my brother."

"I do vaguely remember meeting my great grandmother once. The only thing that stands out in my mind was the smell of her rose perfume. It was like she bathed in it. When my mother, brother and I moved into this house my mother said she couldn't take the smell of roses that seemed to linger in the house. I couldn't smell it, but my mother seemed repelled by what she said lingered in the house. After a few months of living here we moved out. She just put the house in her will for me and it has sat here empty since then."

"That's funny that you say that because when I came in there seemed to be an odor of cherry tobacco in the air."

"Not possible, the Captain was the only one who used to smoke cherry tobacco in this house and he has been long gone."

"I tell you I smell it don't you?"

"Not a whiff must be your imagination."

Chapter Five

After hours of deliberation Ali and Beau finally made a deal. For whatever reason Beau could not just dump the house on her. Call it manly pride, or the fact that he truly enjoyed her company, they managed to set up a deal that would benefit each of them.

"What about your brother, won't he want a say in all of this?"

"No, he said he doesn't care what I do with the property. He doesn't even want a share of it. I will share it with him, even though he said that. I don't want you to think I am greedy." He said nervously as she signed the paperwork he had waiting for her.

Ali was going to pay for all the renovations on the house. After she did this, if she still wanted to buy the house he would sell it to her for the set price that they had determined.

If at the end she decided that she didn't like the house, or if she found that the stories regarding it being haunted were too much, he would pay her back for the renovations, minus a rental fee for the time she spent there. This way the house would be renovated and he would not have to deal with that part, while she gained a place to live and write her next book.

Now that the papers were signed she had to go back and deal with Joe. She got in the car and traveled to the apartment. She had briefly talked to him and she could only hope that he had not thrown her stuff out. She did have some things that had belonged to her grandmother and she definitely wanted them back.

She walked up the stairs and knocked on the door, remembering the last time, she made sure she did not use her keys. He opened the door.

"Well the wandering pilgrim has decided to come home?" He said sarcastically.

"Don't start Joe; I am only here to pack up my things."

"You don't have to work too hard; Natalie boxed most of it up for you."

"Natalie so is that her name, or is this someone new?

"Don't be so crude Ali."

"Wonderful, Well, I hope that the two of you are very happy together."

"Unlike you at least she is here."

Ali nodded her head. She refused to take the blame for his indiscretion. All she wanted was for this to be over.

"So you found a place I guess?"

"Yes, I did, it is a big old Victorian house on the ocean."

"That must come with a pretty big price tag, being on the ocean and all. Your new book a big hit?"

"It's doing ok, enough for me to rent with the option to buy on this place. At least this way I will get something that will eventually belong to me."

"Cute Ali but your sarcasm is wasted on me."

"Where are the boxes? I will start loading them."

"There in the hallway."

"Great, tell Natalie thanks for boxing the stuff up."

"Yeah, well I am going back to watch the game. Go ahead and look around but I think she put everything of yours in the boxes."

So this was it, the end of the so called relationship. For everything she had been through with this guy she wasn't feeling so bad about the break up. She would sure be a lot more careful in whom she chose next time, if there was a next time.

She was sure that at this point old maid sounded pretty good to the heartbreak of lost loves. Her whole life was packed up in twelve boxes. How sad was that? She put the boxes in the car and headed back to her new home. She would have to call Eddie and see if he could get her a deal on a SUV. Her days of red mustangs and fast men were over. She was going to be a home owner and live in solitude in a large rambling mansion overlooking the ocean.

"I hope I don't get so depressed that I jump off the cliff." She said to herself as she drove down the interstate.

*****

"Eddie, listen, Eddie please listen. I am not crazy. I know Eddie, you think that I bought this place to curl up and hide but it is not true. It's a great place and you have to come up and see it."

"Catherine is going to have a fit when she finds out you have moved out of the city."

"Catherine is not in charge of me. I am in charge of me, and where I live, and who I see."

"You're seeing someone? Really are you seeing someone? If you are than I would feel better about all of this. Unless he is another dork, then I will be worried again."

"Eddie, calm down. I am fine."

"You know that I worry about you. This is not like you to take all these chances and what in the world were you thinking buying a house? We can try getting you out of the deal."

"I don't want out of the deal Eddie. I love the house and you need to come and see it. I know you will love it too."

"Nope, I don't think I will love it. I think some jerk has taken you to the cleaners again."

"Not this time Eddie. It feels just right this time."

"You said that last time about Joe and look where that led?"

"Beau is different and he is honest, he wouldn't cheat me. I am sure of it."

"I don't know Ali; he talked you into buying a huge, stupid mansion. Something he has probably been trying to dump on someone for years."

"Eddie stop, it is going to be ok. I just need you to look into getting me a local repair guy who can come in and renovate some of the things in the house. Can you do that for me?"

"Of course I can do that, I am not stupid. I will get right on it."

"Thanks Eddie, you're a doll."

*****

The phone rang as Ali carried in the last of the groceries.

"Hello, my name is Jerry, Jeremiah Longworth actually. I received a call that you might need a handyman.

I have worked in the area before with the local contractor and I can do pretty much everything that most people need. A guy named Eddie said that you wanted to renovate a house."

"That is great, I live at 2555 Ravenswood Cliff, and I am going to need a lot of help to get this house back into shape."

"Did you say Ravenswood Cliff?"

"Yes, is that a problem?"

"Nope, just wondering if you are aware of the history? There are a lot of stories about that place. The locals say it is haunted by the Captain and his wife."

"If you are afraid of these so called stories Mr. Longworth, don't bother to come. I need someone who is dependable and doesn't believe in the ghost stories that have been spread about my house."

"Have you stayed there alone yet?" He asked. "It is different when you're in the house alone. Others have tried to live there you know."

"A couple nights and they were gone. Didn't Beau tell you he has had some difficulty selling the place? If not you can still back out."

"I have no intention of backing out. I will be staying here alone tonight, and for your information I am not afraid of some crazy imaginary ghost." She shook her head thinking what a jerk.

"I will call you tomorrow then, if you're still interested in the place after spending a night in the place alone, I will come and do your renovations."

"Great, then I will talk to you tomorrow morning."

"Talk to you then."

Jeremiah laughed to himself. She won't last the night in that place. What a joke, she actually wants to renovate Ravenswood Manor.

Chapter Six

First thing she was going to have to do was get the furnace fixed she thought as she carried in several loads of firewood. The old fireplaces were nice looking but they left a lot to be desired in the draft area and bringing in enough wood was tiresome.

She started a fire and soon it was toasty warm, at least in the living room. The rest of the house was ice cold. She went into the kitchen to look for something to eat. After searching around the kitchen she soon realized that outside of the few staples she had picked up at the local grocery, and the few old jars of unrecognizable items in the pantry, she had no real food in the house. She picked up her phone, and dialed the nearest Pizza place. Surely they would come and deliver her a pizza and pop.

"Hi, Casey's Pizza how can I help you?"

"Yeah I would like a large pizza, double cheese, pepperoni and a bottle of pop delivered please."

"What's the address?"

"2555 Ravenswood Cliff "she said.

"I'm sorry did you say Ravenswood Cliff? This isn't a prank is it? I mean no one lives at Ravenswood Cliff."

"I am the new owner, and I do live here at Ravenswood Cliff. Now can I get my pizza delivered or not?"

What was it with these people? It was getting a little agitating that people did not believe she lived in this house.

"You would think I was some crazy person for living in this beautiful home." She mumbled under her breath.

"Umm, it will be like forty-five minutes ok? That is if I can get a delivery person to deliver to that house."

"There is nothing wrong with my house. How much will that be?"

"The total is Seven dollars and ninety-nine cents plus a two dollar delivery fee."

"Great I will have it ready when they come."

"Ok" she said while wondering who did she have that would be willing to deliver to that house.

"Hey Mike, want to make a few extra bucks?"

"Sure do, what's the address?"

"Ravenswood Cliff" she looked at him her eyebrows raised waiting for his real answer.

"Are you kidding me?" He paused. "Are you willing to pay me double to go there?" He asked.

"Yes, I guess."

"I don't have to go into the house, right?"

"No, just deliver to the door grab the money and run."

"I guess it will be ok. New owner must be from out of town to not know the history of that place."

"Well, she wants a pizza so can you deliver?"

"Yeah, sure, it will be the fastest delivery in history though."

Ali threw a few more logs on the fire and sat down with her notebook. She was going to have to set up an account for the repairs on the house and work it into her budget. It might take a while but if she put in some hard work herself, by fall she would have a beautiful home she could call her own.

She jotted down the first things she wanted done since it was snowing outside the inside would definitely be the first to get done. She wanted to strip the old wallpaper off the walls and repaint. Then there was the flooring. It would all have to be sanded and re-stained and varnished. A lot of it was cleaning, and then who could forget overhauling the boiler system. Maybe that should be first she thought.

She made up a long list for Mr. Longworth if he decided to show up tomorrow. There was a knock at the door it startled her.

"Oh yes, the pizza" she grabbed her purse and headed to the door. The young man stood there his face was pale white.

"Are you ok?" she asked.

"Yes ma'am here is your pizza and the two liter of pop. That's seven ninety-nine."

"Come in and stay warm while I get you the money. You can put the pizza and pop on the table there."

"I would prefer to stand out here ma'am if you don't mind."

"Ok, but it is senseless to stand out in that cold when it is warm in here."

"That's ok." He stammered as his eyes looked all around the room.

"This is a big place to live in way out here alone" he said.

"I guess so, but I love the peace and quiet of being alone."

"The Captain doesn't bother you?" he asked, as if a ghost had appeared behind her.

"The Captain, you certainly don't mean Captain Ravenswood do you? I can't believe that everyone around here thinks a ghost lives among us."

"Oh he is real ma'am, not a tale, he will show up, and he might not like you living in his house."
"Well…" she paused waiting for him to tell her his name.

"It's Mike, ma'am, and I have lived around here my whole life. Everyone knows about the Captain. I would be careful if I were you. He has been known to have a temper."

"I appreciate your concern Mike, but I am sure I will be just fine. Here is fifteen dollars you keep the change for coming out here on such a cold night."

"Thank you ma'am, anytime you want pizza delivered just tell them you want Mike to deliver."

"No problem. Thanks again for coming out in this yucky weather."

She closed the door and almost laughed as she watched him run to his car and speed away as fast as he could.

"I wonder just what has that boy so scared."

She went to the kitchen to get a glass and some ice. When she returned she noticed that the pizza box was on the coffee table and not the hall table where she had placed it. Surely her eyes must be playing tricks on her. Ok, maybe she hadn't paid attention; maybe she had placed it on the coffee table. She shook her head, grabbed the box, and plopped down on the couch. She poured herself a glass of pop and opened up the box. The smell of pizza permeated the room. This was just what she needed for a cold winters night, pizza, pop and a good movie.

She turned on the TV and hit the DVD player. She was going to watch her favorite old sappy movie starring Cary Grant "An Affair to Remember."

He was a man's man, an epic hero, someone who would never be cruel to a woman, why couldn't she find someone like him, tall, romantic, and handsome?

It had been a long tedious day, her eyes grew heavy, and soon she was fast asleep on the couch. The fire crackled and sputtered as he entered the room.

There she was he could hardly believe it, his beautiful Lizzie just as lovely as the day when hc last saw her. He moved closer to her his hand touching her face. She shivered as his cold hand moved across her cheek.

"My sweet love" he whispered. "You have finally returned at last. Tell mc please that you still love me Lizzie" but trying as hard as he could, she could not hear him.

The afghan floated across the room from the chair as he placed it over her. He bent and kissed her forehead.

"Soon my love, I will be stronger. Soon you shall be able to see me, and hear me. It is you, and only you that have brought my soul back to life once more."

He walked to the fireplace and lit his pipe. The smell of cherry tobacco filled the room.

"It is so good to have you home my love, Mary shall never keep us apart again."

A large vase flew across the room. It crashed into pieces on the stone floor by the fireplace.

"What was that?" 'Ali screamed awakened by the crash.

"How in the world did that vase fall off the mantel by itself?"

She got up from the couch and went to the kitchen to get a broom and dustpan. She was extremely tired but she cleaned up the mess and decided that she would go upstairs to sleep. She would use the master bedroom, after all it was the largest, and had a bathroom attached. She pulled the dust cover sheet off the bed and just crawled under the covers. She was just too tired to worry about anything else until morning.

"I will just do the rest in the morning after a good night's rest and Good Night Captain wherever you are."

He watched her crawl under the covers and soon she was sound asleep.

"I will let you rest my dear. We will have plenty of time to reacquaint ourselves."

Chapter Seven

The light came in through the window shining right across her face. She knew she had to get up soon. The room was ice cold and she hated even getting out from under the blankets, but Mr. Longworth would be arriving to meet with her about the renovations. She definitely decided to have him start with the heating system. It would be the most expensive thing she would have to do so she figured she would get it out of the way first.

She went into the master bathroom and found out quickly that the plumbing in this house was ancient too. There was no shower only an old bear claw bathtub, and when she turned on the water the pipes banged and clanked away. This was just great, how did she ever miss that in the run through of the house with Beau. Well that was going to put her back another fortune. Her books had better sell well and fast.

She was beginning to think that maybe she jumped the gun on leasing to purchase and renovating this monster of a house. It could easily take all the money in her account.

"Stop whining" she told herself out loud. "A bubble bath is just what I need."

She had to use some shampoo to make the bubble bath.

"I am going to sit and relax and try to keep my mind off the crazy thing I have done. Maybe Eddie is right, maybe I have lost it."

As she soaked in the tub she thought it might be amusing to visit Pearl later today after she met with Mr. Longworth and got him started on the renovations. Maybe Pearl would be able to tell her just what this mysterious Captain was thinking about having her in his home. After all she didn't need a mad ghost.

Since the entire town seemed to believe he existed, maybe the Captain would take it upon himself to reveal himself to her. Then either she would become one of the crazies like the rest of the town, or she would become a true believer.

She finished up and dressed just in time as a loud knock came at the front door. It must be Mr. Longworth she thought as she ran down the stairs.

She opened the door and there he stood with his long blond hair dangling in his eyes that were captivatingly blue.

"Hi, I am Jeremiah; I am assuming that you are Ali? Eddie told me what you would look like but he certainly didn't fill me in on just how pretty you are."

"Well Mr. Longworth, welcome to my world, I am hoping that you are as handy as they come because there are a lot of things wrong with this place, and we need to start with the heating."

‘Heating sounds like a good place to start, especially since it is bitterly cold out. Also please call me Jeremiah, I hate being formal.”

“Ok Jeremiah, let’s go this way then.”

She led him to the stairway that led into the basement area. It was dark, cold, and damp. She didn’t like the feelings that seemed to surround her when she went down there to try and get the old furnace to turn on.

“It’s ok you know, to feel the way you are feeling. That is just the captain making his presence known.”

“How do you know how I am feeling?”

“Well, it could be, because I have personally felt the same way many times before. You are not the first person to try and renovate this old house you know? I have done a lot of work in this house in the past.”

“Really, so you have met the so called Captain?”

He hesitated at his answer. "Let's just say that I have felt his presence, just like many others have in the past." He seemed to be picking his words very carefully.

"I would dare to presume that he is here. Most sense his presence but few see him. Maybe, he likes you, and wants you to stay? Rumors have it that others have run screaming from this house."

"You are just teasing me aren't you?"

"Well, maybe a little." He laughed at the expression on her face. "I just wanted to see what you would do."

"Well first of all I don't scare easy, so Mister ghostly Captain may have met his match with me."

"Well, let's go check out this old boiler, and see if we can get you some heat generating in this place."

"That sounds really nice" as she pulled her sweater tighter.

*****

"Aunt Pearl, what is the matter."

"Nothing dear, it is just the Captain. He seems to be in a mood this morning."

"Isn't that his normal?" she chuckled wondering if her Aunt would ever truly admit that all of this ghost stuff was just a ruse to keep bringing in ghost hunting guests.

"Oh no, not this morning Jessica, he seems to be very upset. First, she cannot hear him and he wants to speak with her, and second he wants to keep her away from the cottage. He says he will not allow Jeremiah to stay there. It is a special place and he cannot stay there. It is almost as if he is angered that she has chosen to let him to stay there. "

"Why in the world would he be mad that Jeremiah is staying with Ali, Aunt Pearl? He is perfectly harmless."

"He is jealous of course; he thinks Ali is his precious Lizzie."

"Why in the world would he think that?"

"She resembles his Lizzie I suspect. That is why he is allowing her to live at Ravenswood Manor in the first place. If you remember he has never allowed anyone else to stay there. "

"He seems to be drawing power from Ali's strength just like he does from me. Very soon she is going to see the Captain. I certainly hope she is ready."

"Maybe you should warn her then?"

"I am afraid she will not believe me until he appears before her. I can only hope she is ready when he does."

*****

"You're in luck; the old boiler just needed some tender loving care. It should produce some heat for now.

You just turn the knobs on the radiators to heat whatever room you want heated. It will save you money if you don't turn it on in all the rooms."

"Well, for sure I want the living room, the kitchen, and my bedroom. Once I have my office set up then that room too."

"So Ali, shall we sit down and look over your plan?"

"Yes, and we need to figure out what this is going to cost me too."

"Don't worry about me. I love this old house. I would do it for free, but I do need gas money and I have to pay my rent too."

"I would never ask for you to do it for free, but there is a little cottage where I think the caretaker used to stay. We could work out a deal and you could move in there. That is if you're not afraid of the Captain."

Jeremiah laughed.

"You still think he doesn't exist except in the minds of the crazy people of this town. You will see in time he will reveal himself. It has been said that he gathers strength from those that he chooses. Then when the time is right he reveals himself to them. If others come that he has not chosen well, he chases them out by his ghostly antics."

"What do you mean by ghostly antics?"

"People have seen things move. Ghostly shadows, and definitely the smell of cherry tobacco are evident when he is around."

"You are kidding right?"

"No why, did you see something?"

"I think it is my imagination, just silly talk from people around town you know like Jessica's Aunt Pearl. Last night some strange things happened."

“First I could have sworn I smelled cherry tobacco. Then I thought that I put the pizza box on the table in the hall, but when I came back it was on the coffee table by the couch. I fell asleep on the couch until I was awakened by a vase crashing off the mantel.”

“That sounds more like Mary than the Captain. She loves to move and break things.”

“Plus there was an afghan on me when I woke. I don’t remember covering myself either.”

“I can only guess he is testing you, maybe even welcoming you in his own way. No one has lasted longer than one night in this house.”

“Well, I am not afraid of a ghost, so let him try to get me out of here.”

“That’s, the spirit.” Jeremiah laughed. “Well, how about showing me the caretaker’s place.”

"If it suits my needs, than I will take you up on your offer. I will move in there and take your deal of a weekly salary to take care of all your needs, well most of them anyway. We can talk about what needs to be done later."

The caretaker's house sat in the back off to the side of the main house. It had once been a beautiful cottage. The shutters were hand carved just like the main house, but like everything else they desperately needed to be painted. The weather had made the original paint crack and peal. It needed to be painted and the dust in the cottage had to be at least an inch thick. It had a large living area, kitchen, bedroom, and bath. It was everything Jeremiah needed or so he said. Ali liked the thought of having someone around. Someone that she could depend on if something went wrong. It didn't hurt that he wasn't bad to look at either.

"I would like to start with the cottage if you don't mind. I want to be able to move in as soon as possible so I don't have to pay another month's rent."

"That's fine, to start I just needed heat and you have already taken care of that for me. I have to finish up my book by next week and send it off to my publisher so I will be busy with that. Whenever you finish the cottage you can start on the main house."

"Great I am going to work on this right now."

"If you need me I will be writing, Oh, and the delivery man delivered all the paint it is in the shed with all the painting equipment."

"Ok, I guess we will see each other later then."

"Yes, oh and please join me for dinner tonight. I am making this great beef stew."

"That's a deal; I am not much of a cook myself so a home cooked meal sounds delish."

"See you around six then."

"Six is great."

Chapter Eight

Ali was in the kitchen mixing up biscuits to go along with the beef stew she had on the stove when Jeremiah walked in.

"Wow, looks like you have more paint on you than the walls I think. What happened?"

"I think that maybe the Captain is not happy that I am renovating the cottage."

"Really are you serious?"

"Well a couple paint cans were flying at me. I did manage to finish and clean up the mess, but I am afraid I may not be very welcome here."

"Guess I will have to have a stern talk with the Captain then."

She looked in the air and said. "Captain, if you wish for me to stay here than you have to leave Jeremiah alone."

"He is helping me and if you chase him away I will have no one to help me get this house livable. So stop it now, or I will pack my things and leave. There, how is that."

"I guess we will see." He said laughing at her modest effort to protect him from the captain's antics.

The captain looked at her, he shook his head, yet while he was angry that she said this, he knew she was serious. If he wanted her to stay, he was going to have to leave Jeremiah alone, but he would not do so without giving him a stern warning.

"Ok Lizzie, but if he does anything but keep you safe, he will regret it, and I will chase him as far away as I can."

"Did you hear that?" Ali asked.

"Hear what?"

"I could have sworn I heard a man's voice mumbling. It was really quiet, but I am sure I heard something."

"It must be my imagination." She laughed. "I think you all are getting to me with this Captain stuff."

Jeremiah knew exactly what she was saying. He had seen and heard the Captain loud and clear. The Captain had made his claim and he needed to be careful to not step over the line.

"Well, I am going to get cleaned up if that is ok?"

"Sure no problem, use the master bedroom it has towels and soap on the shelf. There is some shampoo too, which I think you're gonna need."

"Ok," he said giving her a frustrated look. "I should be done in a half hour."

"Dinner should be ready by then."

Ali took in a deep breath as Jeremiah turned and walked out of the kitchen. It was then that the smell of cherry pipe became stronger than ever before.

She looked around the room almost expecting to see someone standing behind her.

"Captain, are you here?" She said hesitantly as she looked around the room again. "I must be crazy listen to me trying to talk to a non-existent ghost. Soon I am going to be as crazy as the rest of this town."

"Sweet Lizzie, with your presence I am getting stronger, and the more you begin to believe the sooner you will see and hear me." He said as he ran his hand across her cheek.

Ali shivered at the chill and grabbed her sweater. "This house is just way to drafty. I am going to have to do something else to eliminate it."

She set up dinner at the dining room table and then yelled upstairs.

"Dinner is ready. Come and get it."

"Be down in a second Ali."

He finished drying himself off and pulled a clean sweater over his head.

The Captain stood at the end of the bed. “Do not touch my Lizzie, do you hear me.” He barked off as Jeremiah looked right into the Captains deep blue eyes

. “You have nothing to worry about Captain; I will take care of her. No one will get close to her. It is my promise to you.”

“She cannot leave me again.”

“Jeremiah!” she called again.

“Are you done yet?”

“I’ll be right down Ali.” He yelled tipping his hand to the Captain. “She will be safe with me I promise you.”

The smell of the beef stew was enticing as he came down the stairs.

“I am as hungry as a bear.”

"Well that's good because I think I made enough stew for six people."

"Well I guess we will have a party then, but I think there aren't too many people who will come here."

"Once this house is done there will be parties galore. I plan to have all my New York friends in for a grand open house."

Jeremiah looked a little concerned. "You're not afraid that the Captain may play some antics if you bring strangers into his house."

"Oh come on, the Captain again? I only did that to appease you in the kitchen. There is no Captain lingering around here."

"If you say so Ali, but I can't believe that the whole town believes in the Captain and you do not."

"Well, once I see him then maybe I will believe."

"You have it all turn around backwards Ali. First you have to believe and then you get to see. That's where your problem is."

Jeremiah sat down at the table and ate as if he hadn't eaten in ages.

"Dinner is great Ali, how did an accomplished book writer become a good cook too?"

"Well, my mother was a chef at the Waldorf hotel for most of my life. We lived at the hotel; it was one of the perks of my mother's job."

"How did you become a writer then?"

"Well, one of the things I did while my mother worked was sit in the lobby of the Hotel. I would make up stories of the people that passed me by. I would look at them and see a story appear before me."

"In that case what kind of story would you write about me?"

"There is a little air of mystery about you. Inquisitive character that has a past he doesn't want to reveal. He hides it behind his beautiful blue eyes and blonde hair. His smile captivates women, yet he is a loner and doesn't act as though he wants any kind of relationship with anyone. How am I doing so far?"

"Not bad." He laughed. He watched the Captain as he sat down at the table beside her. "Mystery part is very correct. I am a person who keeps my private life private. You're good at reading people."

"A writer has to be. I should be more like you. Private I mean. Every time I allow myself to get involved with someone I let myself get vulnerable and then I miss the cues or I tend to ignore them."

“Like with Joe my last boyfriend. I don’t know how I missed his cheating side. I guess I wanted to believe that he loved me enough to be faithful and truthful. Now I think that no man can ever be that way.”

“Don’t give up on all men Ali. Some of us are good inside. We mean well, we just don’t always do the right things. In fact I will show you tonight. I will clean up the kitchen and do the dishes while you relax by the fire with a glass of wine. How is that for being gallant?”

“That would be spectacular. I am so exhausted today. People think that writing is easy. The brain work is so tiring though. I could sleep through a raging storm tonight and not hear a sound.”

"Well tonight is your night. Go sit by the fire in the living room and I will bring you a glass of wine."

Ali got up from the table and went to help take the dishes to the kitchen but Jeremiah stopped her.

"Nope not a dish, go sit and relax."

She was going to definitely enjoy this tonight. She walked into the living room and stirred up the fire a bit in the fireplace as she tossed in a couple more logs. She closed her eyes and again she smelled the cherry tobacco. It had to be something about the house that this smell seemed to follow her everywhere she went. Maybe, just maybe there was something to the ghost of the Captain.

She sat in the chair and put her feet up on the ottoman just as Jeremiah returned with a glass of wine.

"Here you go, relax I have everything under control."

He turned toward the fireplace where the Captain stood he nodded his head toward Jeremiah as if he approved. Jeremiah retreated to the kitchen.

"You are so lovely my dear," the Captain said as if Ali were listening to his words. She took a sip of wine and then relaxed and closed her eyes

. "If only you believed my sweet Lizzie, just how can I make you believe?"

"Hey Jer, forget the dishes and come and join me. You worked hard today. You don't have to do them for me."

"I will be there in a second, I am almost done."

She smiled. What kind of man would work hard all day and then offer to do the dishes? He seemed to be quite different than the men she had met before.

He came back into the room with the wine bottle and a glass for himself. “Want some more?”

“I would love another glass, thank you.”

He poured her another glass and sat on the sofa next to her.

“So Ali, what do you think so far of Ravenswood? Do you think you will stay? I know you and Beau have some kind of deal going on, but what are your true thoughts.”

“I love it here actually. I almost feel like I belong here. It’s almost like I have a connection with this house. Strange don’t you think? I mean I have never been here before, and yet I feel like I have been here my whole life.”

“What about you? Why are you here? Is there some reason that you settled here?”

“Long story Ali, long story.”

“I am all ears. Tell me your story I want to know” she said as she yawned.

“I think it is a story for another night. You’re tired and so am I. I am going to take my leave and head to the cabin for a good night’s sleep. I suggest you head upstairs for the same.

“Ok, I am tired, but you’re not getting out of this so easily. I want the story.”

“I will tell you, I promise. Now go get some sleep.”

He helped her up off the couch and kissed her cheek goodnight.

“See you in the morning Ali.”

Chapter Nine

"Yes Catherine, I know the book tour is this week. I am all ready for it. I have called ahead and it is all set for seven p.m. on Monday. Eddie made all the plans and he will meet me there to help set it up. I don't know what you're all worried about. It is not like it is the first book tour I have done. Yes, I will see you there. Catherine, you are such a worrier."

Ali hung up the phone cursing about everything she had to get together. She was just going to be gone two weeks. It wasn't a lifetime yet even Jeremiah was making a big fuss too. It was almost as if he thought she wasn't coming back. He seemed to be in a panic mode for the last couple days.

"Is everything ready?" he startled her as he stood at the bedroom door.

"Yes, and I will be back in two weeks. I promise." She said as she touched his arm walking out of her room with suitcase in hand.

"Let me carry that for you" he replied. Over the weeks he had become quite attached to Ali. She was a breath of fresh air, someone quite different from any of the women he had met before. He even tried hard to ignore the stern looks he was receiving from the Captain each time he seemed to overstep his boundary. It would be so much easier if she could see the Captain herself, but until then he would have to remain silent.

He placed the suitcase in the back of the SUV and closed the hatch. She looked at him as if she didn't want to go, but she had obligations.

"Jer, I promise I will be back. I am not sure why you are so upset about all this."

"It's really nothing Ali, ignore my idiosyncrasies and go do your book tour. I will be fine."

"I told you that I have to do tours in order to promote my books. If I don't I can't afford to live here, and we both lose our homes."

"Spring is almost here and we are going to have a lot of outside work to do on this house. I will start on my new book and we will have months before I have to do another tour."

He wanted to tell her everything, but she wouldn't believe him anyway. The Captain was glaring at him from behind her. The closer he got the more he saw the anger rising in the Captains face. Ali was getting ready to get into the car when she reached up and pulled Jeremiah down to her level and kissed him. "I will be back."

Out of nowhere he went flying back onto the ground, his head hitting the car as the Captain punched him straight in the face.

"Are you ok?" She cried as she ran and knelt on the ground beside him. "What just happened?"

He just sat there staring back at the Captain.

“I warned you to leave my Lizzie alone, did I not?” he growled at him.

Ali turned her head as she heard the voice. There he stood right in front of her. The Captain, the man in the portrait was shaking his fist as if it hurt.

Ali stared at the Captain said “oh my” and sunk down on the ground next to Jeremiah. She leaned into his arms, took a deep breath, closed her eyes, and fainted. He carried her into the house and laid her on the couch.

“Look what you have done.” The Captain yelled.

“Me, you’re angry at me? You are the one who did this.”

“She saw me though did she not? Now at last my Lizzie has returned to me and she will believe.”

Jeremiah ran to the kitchen to get a cold wet rag to put on her forehead.

"Ali, are you ok?" he asked as he stared sternly back at the Captain.

"Don't look at me that way Jeremiah. Your job was only to keep her safe, and keep her from leaving. You have done neither as far as I can see."

"With your interference it is a wonder she didn't leave ages ago."

"Where am I, what happened? She asked

"You fainted, that's all." He replied.

"Oh I could have sworn I saw the Captain, what a dream." She laughed.

"Not a dream, my sweet Lizzie." The Captain said standing in front of the fireplace smoking his pipe.

She looked up at him and then back at Jeremiah.

"Please tell me that this is a dream."

"Sorry Ali, it is more of a nightmare I think."

"He really exists." She opened the wet cloth and covered her face, leaned back on the couch and moaned.

"It will be ok once you get used to him and his arrogance Ali."

"No, I think not. I think I need to visit Miss Pearl."

"I think you have a book tour first though?"

"Oh my God, I almost forgot. I have to go. I am going to be late and Catherine will be frantic."

"I want to call you a cab instead of you driving what do you say to that? I am not sure it would be safe for you to drive in this condition."

"Yeah, I think your right. I shouldn't drive like this. I need to get myself together. Everyone will all think I am crazy. Shoot, I think I am crazy."

Jeremiah pulled out his phone and ordered a cab. Just then an overwhelming smell of roses entered the room.

"Just look what you have done this time Masterson? When will you learn that Lizzie is gone, and is never returning? Have you not heard Jeremiah? This woman is not your Lizzie. No, but you just keep looking don't you?"

Ali turned her head toward the voice. The woman standing there was most definitely more beautiful than the portrait that hung in the bedroom. Her harsh voice however grated on everyone's nerves. Ali looked at Jeremiah just to make sure that she was not the only one seeing this woman standing in the living room with them.

"She is real too" he said. "Well, as real as he is I should say."

"How long have you been able to see them?"

"A very long time I am afraid."

"Have they always been this obnoxious to each other?"

"I am afraid so, at least for as long as I can remember."

"You need not talk about us in this manner. We are present you know."

"Oh we know, yes we definitely know." he replied

A horn beeped outside the house.

"Your cab is here Ali, you need to go. Get out while you can. I will handle the two of them. Go now while you have a chance, and have a good book tour."

Ali got off the sofa, grabbed her jacket, and almost ran out the door.

"If she ever comes back, you will be really lucky." He looked at the captain

"She will be back, now that she knows I am here. She is my Lizzie, she loves me, she will return."

"All this time, and you are still a pompous piece of work"

"Well said Mary." Jeremiah replied as the Captain and Mary disappeared.

Chapter Ten

Due to the unexpected guests at her home Ali arrived at the bookstore a half hour later than expected. Catherine was already a mess and Eddie was just happy to see her arrive in one piece.

“Ali, are you ok? Why the taxi, didn’t you get the SUV we talked about?”

“I got the SUV Eddie; I was just not capable of driving at the time.”

“Were you drinking? I have warned you about that. I know you are alone but that doesn’t give you an excuse to abuse.”

“Trust me Eddie, when I say I am definitely not alone.”

“Just what is that supposed to mean? Maybe I don’t want to know. Forget it don’t tell me. I definitely do not want to know.”

"Ok, get me up to date, what are we doing here?"

Eddie hustled her off to the table where he had all her new books prominently displayed. This was an evening show and would start at around eight thirty. She was to do a reading of her book and then the book signing would commence. The store was quite a conglomerate of books and much more.

The bookstore had a coffee, snack, and lunch bar along with a wide variety of herbal drinks. At this moment she wished they were all alcoholic. She wondered how many people would even care that she was there for this signing. She couldn't get her mind off Jeremiah. What would be waiting for her when she returned, if she returned?

She hadn't decided if that was what she wanted to do. She liked Jeremiah but he had lied to her. Well, maybe he hadn't but he didn't tell her the truth. Well, maybe he had, maybe she just didn't listen close enough. There was much more to this story and she had never given up on a story before, but this one was freaking her out.

She had to concentrate on tonight and the book tour. It would be at least two weeks before she would have to decide what she was going to do about going home.

He really knew about the Captain and Mary and yet he never told her, well maybe he did but he should have told her more convincingly. Why was that she thought? They had become close, and yet he had kept these secrets. Maybe he thought she would think he was crazy? She probably would have, but did she deserve his dishonesty? Why did this feel so much like a betrayal? Were all men this dishonest maybe she just hadn't noticed before? They had all led her to believe in them. First it was Bill, then Joe, and now him. Then wham, you find out they have these deep secrets they have hidden from you. It was always her belief that if someone really cares about you they don't keep secrets.

The first showing went well she thought. She sold at least a hundred books, she knew she signed at least that many. Catherine seemed well pleased.

Eddie asked her to go to dinner with him and Catherine, but she was too tired.

"It has been quite a hectic day. You guys go ahead I am going to head to bed and think about tomorrows plan."

She went to the hotel and settled into her room. She ordered pizza and once they delivered she sat back on the bed put several pillows behind her and turned on the TV. Tomorrow would be the same scenario, just a different bookstore. Maybe doing the same thing tomorrow would help. She would keep a strict regimen with no distractions. She would be crazy busy, and it was probably for the best it would keep her mind off of the ghostly duo waiting for her at home.

She picked up her phone several times to call Jeremiah but chickened out. What would she say? Hey, how are the captain and his wife? Are they still chilling out at the house? My god, I am going crazy she thought.

Then she panicked. What about him? Would he be ok alone with the ghostly duo? She had to call him if nothing more than to make sure he was ok.

"Hello" he answered with the deep voice she had gotten to know so well in the past few weeks.

"Hi" she replied. "Are you ok? I mean I left in such a hurry that I didn't even think about the fact that I left you alone with uhh them."

He chuckled. She was worried about him. How cute he thought. He didn't remember anyone being worried about him before.

"I am just fine Ali. I haven't seen either of them since you left."

“Thank God, I was so worried and feeling guilty about leaving you there alone, especially after the captain hit you. Why did he hit you?”

“Long story and it can wait until you return. I will fill you in when you get back.”

“Are you sure you’re going to be ok there alone?”

“Yes, and I have lots of work to keep me busy. I will have a nice surprise ready for you when you return.”

“Really, what kind of surprise do you have for me?”

“Ali, it wouldn’t be a surprise if I told you.”

“Haven’t I told you I am really bad at surprises?”

“You may have said that a time or two, but you are not changing my mind.

I really should be asking you if you’re ok. I know that all of this is weird but I wasn’t sure how to get you to believe me.”

"Yeah, I am not sure I would have really believed it even if you had stood there and told me he was standing there. I mean Aunt Pearl told me, and I thought she was crazy too. I guess I owe her a big apology. It's that, or maybe I am the one that has gone crazy."

"No Ali, you're not crazy. Beau should have told you, but he saw dollar signs and figured by the time you realized it you would own the house. He wouldn't have to worry about dumping it on someone else. You would have to figure out what to do."

"So, Beau did this to me then. I guess some more negotiations should be done now that all this has surfaced."

"Maybe so Ali, maybe so" he said looking forward to her next confrontation with him.

"So Jeremiah, what do I do?"

“There is time to figure it out.”

“How is the book tour going? Are you selling lots of books?”

“Well, its uneventful that’s for sure, but Catherine and Eddie seem pleased with the results so far.”

“Are the dynamic duo still there?”

“Nah, actually after you left they both left too. It has actually been peaceful here.” He laughed.

“Well, I will be back in two weeks.” She was hesitant as she asked the most important question

. “They can’t travel too far from the house right? They aren’t going to just show up here right?” she said very anxiously looking around the room.

“Well the truth is I am not sure. They may be able to go to places that they went while they were alive. The house however is their main power station so to speak.”

"Oh great, even if I do ever get used to them I will never be able to invite anyone over to the house."

"How about if we worry about that part when the time comes? For now, enjoy your trip."

"Yeah, enjoy. I guess so. We're heading to California tomorrow. Jeremiah?" she stopped mid-sentence.

"Yes?" he answered.

"Never mind, we can talk when I return."

Chapter Eleven

He was agitated that morning; Mary had gone out of her way to make his last night home miserable for him. Matthew had been sick, and she was never the care giver type. She always dealt that out to Lizzy. He was unable to meet with Lizzy as they had planned because of it. She had been hinting for several days that it was important and that she needed speak to him. There were so many things to do to get ready for this voyage he had put her off. Now that he had time she was busy caring for Matthew.

The next morning at the dock made it even worse. He regretted that he had been so harsh with her. The cracked boom, along with the hangover he had from his binge the night before didn't fare well.

"Alexandra," he barked at her knowing if he used her first name she would get the point that he was angry for the interruption.

"We will talk about all of it as soon as I return, it cannot be that important." He said harshly not considering her feelings at all.

Not realizing that this would be the last conversation he would have with her.

The hurt look on her face as she held back her tears was the last memory he had stuck in his head now. A memory that would haunt him eternally, he had to find her, tell her he was sorry.

When he returned and found that she had vanished into thin air he went on a drunken binge that lasted for weeks. His plan to take her away was over and he was stuck in Ravenswood.

Mary was making his life miserable. She had tried desperately to find someone to take Lizzie's place as chambermaid and nursemaid.

The old woman she had hired to replace Lizzy was at least fifty years old. That was only one of the ways she had to torture him.

"Don't you think you are carrying this way too far Masterson? She left of her own free will you know. Maybe it has been all for the best we need to move on. My father was beginning to catch on that there was something going on between the two of you."

"There was nothing going on between us that haven't already gone on between you and every available merchant in town." He yelled back loud enough for all in the household to hear.

"How dare you accuse me of cavorting with men while you are at sea?"

"Accuse? Really Mary, everyone knows it is the town gossip at the local tavern. They even question if Matthew really belongs to me.

It seems it is a toss-up between me and Mr. Carver Williams. So tell me sweet devoted wife. Is Matthew really mine? You claim so, but even I am not sure."

"How dare you say that? Of course Matthew is yours."

"Well, it wouldn't be the first time you have lied to me sweet Mary."

"How dare you accuse me of such things? I am going to take an extended trip to my Aunt's home in Delaware. I cannot live with a man who accuses me of doing something that he himself has done multiple times in our marriage without thought."

He couldn't argue with that, he had been with many women hoping that each one would somehow wipe out Mary from his existence.

"Do not bring anyone into this conversation about you." He blasted back at her.

“You must mean your sweet little innocent Lizzie then.”

His anger was rising at the mention of her name, and Mary knew just what buttons to push him over the edge.

“Just what do you mean by that?” he barked back.

“Really, well then why do you think she left here in secret and disgrace?”

He looked at her wondering what she meant by that statement. She was not like other women in this town who slept with every available man in town, including his wife.

“Well, my dear she had obviously been with some man. She would never admit who he truly was. She was protecting some married man I am sure. It probably was one of your drunken friends who raped her, since she never gave anything freely.” She said sarcastically.

“One of your cronies deprived me of a nursemaid, and I was stuck taking care of Matthew day and night.”

"That is a mother's job you do know that Mary? Although I would never really call you a caring devoted mother."

"How dare you say those words to me Masterson? I was forced to go through carrying your child, and the pain of delivery that ripped me apart, and destroyed my maidenly body just so that you could brag to the men about your male prowess."

"Really Mary, is that all? Go then you disgust me with your rantings. Leave my son, and go."

"No Masterson, you do not win that easily. I will go but your son goes with me. You can live out the rest of your life pining for your sweet Lizzie, never knowing what happened to her. There was a lot of talk you know. Things that I had to go through as your name was dragged through the mud, and mentioned among the possible fathers. It was only when Charlie admitted that it was his child that everything finally died down.

Lizzie never confirmed that it was Charlie though. So that led to a lot of speculation and gossip."

Masterson took a step back. It couldn't be. She loved him. If Charlie or one of his cronies had raped her she would have told him immediately. It couldn't possibly be what she had wanted to tell him that night, or the morning before he left.

Yet, if what Mary was saying was true and it was his child she would have surely told him, she wouldn't have hesitated.

He had played this over and over in his head. It was only one night, a night he would never forget. They had gone to the cottage to be alone, to hide from the rest of the world. It had been raining that night and she was soaking wet. He had insisted that she disrobe and hang her wet clothes by the fire to dry.

It wasn't supposed to happen but her beauty, and his desire was more than his body could handle. He would never forgive himself if she went through all this disgrace because of him and his desire to possess her that night. There was no way that the father could be Charlie.

It was that night he decided he would do whatever it took to be with her. It had to be what she was trying to tell him that day on the dock. He had pushed her away as if she meant nothing more than a possession that he had acquired. If he forced her into Charlie's arms to save face he would never forgive himself.

He must find her no matter what. He would search forever to find out the truth, to make things right.

*****

She stood on the dock watching him sail off once more. How many times had she watched him go wondering if he would ever return?

Each time he returned he would present her with a gift. The best gift was the silver locket he gave her. He had painstakingly place pictures of the two of them in it as children. She would forever hold it close to her heart. This time it was harder than ever before, watching the ship sail out of the cove.

She knew that she would have to leave before he returned. Maybe it was best that she had not told him the news she had.

He would eventually get over her leaving, but if he knew she was carrying his child, then he would never give up looking for her. If the mistress of the house found out the truth she would not only be fired but probably placed in jail for the debt her parents still owed. She would remain as long as she could. She knew that as soon as the baby would start to show she would have to leave.

She would miss Matthew. He was a beautiful child and she loved him dearly, but her safety was foremost and Matthew would survive and forget her eventually.

She would have her own child to remember the love she and Masterson shared. Masterson would be the one to suffer most because he would never know what really happened. Their child was the most important thing to her and she had to protect it.

She would never allow her child to live in ridicule, or be sentenced like her to a life of servitude. The tears flowed down her face as she walked away from the dock. She was on her own and it would not be easy. The stables were a place that she always felt content. It was quiet and peaceful there and the horses always listened intently to her plight. They would listen without ridicule and shame.

"Shadow, what I am going to do?" she asked tearfully as she patted his face. "I am going to have a child and I have no husband to help me." She wiped her eyes with her sleeve.

Charlie McPherson was the son of the man who ran the stables. He was several years older than Lizzie. He had come with his parents from Ireland just like her. They were in the same kind of situation when it came to the debts that were owed for their passage from Ireland. Charlie felt they were more like slaves than hired help and had mentioned it many times in passing. He had suffered some severe beatings for his outspoken words.

Mistress Westwood's father was the real tyrant that kept them enslaved. He had paid for their passage to the America's and somehow managed to keep them constantly in debt. Room and board was always more than what they earned, so nothing ever got paid off it just added up to more debt.

He stood by the stable door and heard Lizzie crying. She was sweet and gentle and it broke his heart to see her so distraught. He walked in behind her.

"Lizzie, can I help?" he asked.

"You were spying on me?" she cried out in anger. Now she would have to do something faster. If Charlie knew soon the whole staff would know.

"No, I am not spying on you. I want to help. Who does your child belong to?" he asked pretty much knowing that it was Masterson. He had watched them growing up and saw where the relationship was heading. He always knew it would end up tragically for Lizzie, but he had hoped she would land on her feet.

She was the strongest person he knew. She could hold her ground to the best of them.

A true Irishwoman he would say, feisty and headstrong, and a true match for any Irishman. Mistress Mary would be the only one that had the capacity to destroy what Lizzie really wanted in life.

"Never mind Lizzie, a man would be blind to not know who the father of your child is."

"If you know than so will everyone else. I have to go. I have to pack my things and go now, before anyone knows the truth."

"Stop Lizzie, think about what it is you are saying. If you run they will all know the truth, but if you marry me, I will help you. I promise I will raise your child as if it were my own. We can leave together. The gossip will be about us and not Masterson. It is the best plan. You and I will get out of this place and be on our own. No one will know anything. They will think the child is mine."

"It will kill Masterson."

"No, Lizzie, it will save him. Think about it. We can run together as husband and wife and no one will ever own us again."

Lizzie knew he was right. She could stay, but it would end up badly for both her and Masterson. She could not destroy the man she loved. She had to leave.

Having Charlie with her would mean she would be safe and not alone. It was the right thing to do.

Chapter Twelve

"Ali, did you get everything?"

"Yes Eddie, I did. I gathered all the info and we did quite well with this tour. We sold over 50,000 books and it is in the top 10 of the best seller listing in New York. I never thought it would make it that high."

"You need to get started on your next book quick so that we can go with the momentum of Castaway Cove. They seem to like that pirate stuff right now."

"I have been thinking about going in a different direction though."

"No way Ali, you have to continue on this route for now. You can't change it up now. The books are hot and we have to kindle that flame by going on. What's with you anyway? You have been in this foggy mood the entire trip. Usually you're the party girl and instead you have been in the hotel room by nine o'clock every night."

"I have had a lot on my mind the last few weeks."

"It seems as though since you bought that big old house your concentration has been elsewhere."

"It's an interesting old place Eddie, you would love it."

"Well, try inviting me there then."

"I will but for now I can't. I want the house to be perfect before I invite anyone over." What she really meant was only if the Captain and Mary were gone. She couldn't take the chance that the ghostly duo wouldn't wreak havoc with her friends.

"Does it have to do with your handyman? I mean you haven't said much about him, only that he rescued you."

"I said he rescued me? I don't remember saying that."

"Well, it might have been you talking in your sleep in the cab that night."

"Oh brother, I do not talk in my sleep."

"I beg to differ with you. You mentioned the Captain and how he was disrupting your life."

"I did not." She said adamantly. There was no way that she could reveal to Eddie or Cat about the Captain and Mary. They would think she had lost it.

"I am just anxious to get back home and do the rest of the renovations on the house. When that is all done I will invite you I promise."

"Don't let him see your fingers crossed behind your back." She jumped at the words. The Captain was suddenly sitting in between them in the cab. She held her tongue as he smiled at her.

“Lizzie this man is not for you at all. He is a peony, a small flower in the garden of men. You can’t be serious about inviting him to dinner at the house.”

“How many times do I have to tell you I am not Lizzie?” She whispered back.

“Ali, you say something?”

“No nothing Eddie, I was just thinking out loud.”

“Well, we are almost to the airport, so New York here we come. It will be wonderful to get back to the big city.”

“What in the world? There is definitely something wrong with this boy, weren’t you just in a big city? He must be some sort of dunce?”

“Dunce?” she said looking at the Captain with a horrified face.

“Did you say something Ali, my earphones were in I didn’t hear what you said.”

"It was nothing Eddie, nothing at all."

Just then her cell phone rang.

"Hey Ali, do you want me to pick you up at the airport. If so when does your plane get in?"

He could tell by her voice that something was not quite right.

"Are you ok Ali?"

She looked at Eddie; he had already put his ear buds back in his ears, so she could safely say what she wanted to say.

"It seems that maybe the Captain has traveled a lot more in his lifetime than we knew if what you told me was true."

"I told you he can only go where he has been during his lifetime, however I am gathering from the sound of your voice that he has paid you a visit?"

"Oh I think so." She said sarcastically.

"Who is that Ali?" Eddie asked.

"My friend Jeremiah, he wants to pick me up at the airport."

"I see, I guess that means that drinks with me are out?"

"Maybe next time Eddie." Eddie was sweet but the captain may have been right in his assumptions. He was a peony in the man classification. Oh brother, she thought now the captain was deciding what men she should or should not be attracted too. This just had to stop. The car pulled into the airport and she gathered her suitcase and headed in to the check in.

"Ali, wait up." Eddie yelled while she tried to finish her private conversation with Jeremiah.

"I am sorry Ali, I really am. I didn't think he would follow you that far. I was sure that he drew his strength from the house."

"Well, he made it uncomfortable, but he didn't stay long, so maybe there is something to that philosophy. I will be at the airport around ten; do you think you can meet me there? I would much rather come home than stay alone at a hotel."

"Yeah, I will be there."

There had to be more to this than what Jeremiah suspected. There was a reason that the Captain was stalking Ali, and he had to figure out what it was, before something tragic happened to her. The Captains existence beyond the grave was his families curse and it was up to him to end it. He just had to figure out what attracted him so much to Ali. There had to be something there that caused his reappearance.

It had been years and now here he was again, and this time he brought Mary with him. It was obvious she did not wish to be there with him, yet everything seemed to be tied to Ravenswood Manor.

……

Jeremiah was standing at the luggage deck waiting for Ali to appear. When he saw her his heart beat a little faster. She was beautiful, he could understand the Captains feelings but he was dead, so why the obsession with her?

"Ali, I'm over here." He shouted.

She smiled when she saw him and put her finger in the air that she would be there in one minute. She had to pick up her suitcase. He walked over toward the conveyer belt to stand next to her.

"There it is the one with the purple ribbon attached."

"Purple ribbon?" he asked.

"Of course, how many people do you think would put a purple ribbon on their suitcase? I would find it in a flash this way."

"Smart move Ali, I would never have thought of that."

"When you travel as much as I do you want to find your luggage fast and get out as soon as you can."

They laughed as he quickly grabbed it off the belt for her. "Is this it?"

"That's it. Let's go. I am tired and I want to go home."

"Uh, yeah about home…" He stammered.

"Why is it that I am thinking I will not like this at all?"

"My surprise was a little bit delayed, and although you will love it. You can't walk on the floors until tomorrow."

"You did the floors?"

"Yep, I did and they look great. You could stay at the cottage with me though. If you want to that is? I promise it will be safe."

"Ok, let's do that then. We will camp out at the cottage."

"Great! I mean that in the most sincere way. You know that right?"

"Yeah, right" She was tired and even if it meant sleeping on a hard couch or floor she didn't care. She just needed sleep.

Chapter Thirteen

There wasn't much conversation on the ride home. Jeremiah filled her in on what he had been doing around the house. He was hoping that she would be pleased with what he had done so far. There was some wall painting to do but he didn't want to start any of that without discussing the color scheme she wanted. He had argued that red was way too harsh for the dining room walls, but he figured with her spunk he was going to lose that battle.

She slept soundly and except for a few words now and then she looked peaceful.

"Why do you continue to call me Lizzie?" she said in her sleep.

He wondered what she meant by that. Who was calling her Lizzy? He was going to remember to ask her in the morning. Maybe it had something to do with the Captain.

It could be a clue to why he was still haunting the house. Maybe Ali was right when she said they should make a visit to Aunt Pearl. It seems that Jessica's Aunt Pearl knows the most about the story behind Ravenswood Manor.

As he drove down the road he saw the light from the lighthouse shining across the waves. He stopped the car and could swear there was a ship in the cove. He walked closer to the cliff. He was almost on the edge. The sail was different from any ship he had seen before, and he knew most of them having grown up by the cove. It was almost transparent there was an object in the center but it was to pale to make out. If it weren't for the light he would have missed it totally. He closed his eyes for a second as the light shined in his face. When he opened his eyes the ship was gone.

"I know that I am tired, but I could not have imagined that?"

"Are we home," Ali said as she moved up next to him on the cliff. "What are you staring at?"

"I am not sure you would believe me if I told you."

"Me, you think I won't believe you?" she laughed leaning against him. "After my encounter with the Captain and Mary I would pretty much believe anybody."

He felt it best that he not tell her this one though. There was some investigation that definitely had to be done. Hopefully she was going to be up to it in the morning.

"Let's get settled" he said as they walked to the cottage together.

"He will regret this action" the captain mumbled as he watched Jeremiah walk Ali to the cottage.

"You can have the bed, I will take the couch." He said as he pulled out a blanket and pillow and threw it on the couch in the living room.

“Are you sure? I am much shorter than you and will fit on the couch better.”

“Nope, I would not be a gentleman if I did that.”

“Well, I won’t complain then because I am exhausted. The time change is having havoc with my body.”

“Sleep tight Ali” he said. He sat down on the couch and decided he would pull out one of the books on the shelf to read. He had never seen a ship like that before. He had lived here his whole life and not one resembled that ship.

He pulled out a couple books that looked somewhat interesting to him. They were pretty old and one almost looked as if it were a journal. He opened it up and started reading. Fortunes are made and lost by the sleight of hand. If only my son were smart enough to see that what I do is all for his future.

The treasures he brings back can of course be sold but it will not last. He laughs at me when I say the pirates will take their portion and soon we will be left with nothing. If he doesn't marry soon, he will wind up being no one in a world of no ones. I have worked too hard for him to give it all up for a servant girl. I regret the day I brought them back from Ireland. I should have left them in that poor village to starve to death, but my wife she could not bear it.

Jeremiah glanced forward in the book and noticed it was not just a book it was a journal written by the captain's father, old man Ravenswood. As he read on he learned that the Wentworth family was relentless in their quest for owning every shipping and importing business on the east coast. The Wentworth family had suffered many losses at sea by so called renegade pirates.

For some reason though Masterson and the Ravenswood family, didn't seem to have that kind of problem. Old man Ravenswood not too much unlike his son was a drinking and gambling man.

His losses at the poker table were becoming well known. As much as Masterson brought in plenty of treasure, his father's loss at the table hurt the business greatly. It was a definite cause of argument and anger between father and son.

Owing the Wentworth's a great deal of money Robert Wentworth gave Ravenswood an ultimatum. Join their families together, or go down with the rest of the companies they would soon be taking over.

Robert admired Ravenswood's son Masterson. He was handsome and smart, but he had a secret when he was at sea. He could bring in any load of treasure and no one seemed to touch what was on his ship.

The Wentworth's were determined to find out what it was that he did that prevented anyone from ever raiding his fleet of ships.

Being a part of the family would certainly bring a wealth of knowledge to the business, and the two families would take over the entire east coast. Jeremiah put the book down. There was so much more to this story than even he had been told. He wondered if Ali would mind if he went to see Aunt Pearl with her. Maybe she held the answer to all of this mystery.

He got up and walked to the bedroom door. Ali laid there her hair in curls around her face and spread out on the pillow. She was the most beautiful sight he had ever seen. He could understand why the captain was fascinated by her, but there was more to it than this. Maybe there would be more in the journal but he was tired.

He pulled the quilt up over Ali and headed back to the couch. He lay down and looked at the stars in the sky outside the window. What were the captain's secrets? How did he manage to sail the seas and avoid the pirates that seemed to plague everyone else? What did all of it have to do with Ali, because something had to do with her?

Chapter Fifteen

Ali woke and wondered where she was. "How did I get here" she asked herself. "Oh yeah, Jeremiah I almost forgot."

The smell of bacon came lusciously wafting through the doorway from his small kitchen. "Is that food I smell?" she asked hoping he was cooking for two.

"Yes, it is." He replied. "I made some French toast and coffee, both of which I think you need."

"Oh I love you, not only a handyman but a chef too. My world is complete."

"I have such a headache did we drink last night?"

"Not that I know of, I think it is just jet lag."

"Oh yeah that's right. Just give me coffee for now."

"Here you go." He handed her a cup of black coffee. She took it from him and drank it down as if she was a dying man in a desert for a week with no water.

"Whoa, that coffee is hot you know that right?"

"Yes, I do" she replied as she sucked on her burning tongue.

"I know that you said you wanted to see Jess's Aunt Pearl when you got back. Did you plan to do that today? I would like to go along if it's ok with you?" he hesitated hoping she didn't think he was interfering with her investigation. He had more at stake than he wanted to admit in finding out some of the answers.

"Sure I don't mind if you go with me. I would like to look at the floors though after all if you put all that work into this house I want to appreciate it."

"You are funny, you know that."

"Not many say that, but I do try once in a while."

“Finish eating, I am going to take a shower and get dressed and when you’re ready we can look at the floors and then go see Aunt Pearl.”

“Great.” She grabbed the fork and plastered the French toast with butter and syrup and ate as if she was starving. First the coffee, and now this she must not have had anything to eat while she was gone he thought. She wasn’t sure why she was so hungry, but whatever was causing it had to stop. Nerves, that’s what it was just nerves. Having Jeremiah around was one thing, but waiting for the next visit from the captain had her on edge. When she was nervous she tended to eat.

*****

“Are you ready to go?” he yelled from the other room. “Let’s head to Aunt Pearl’s first you can check out the floors later.”

“Be ready in one minute” she said as she grabbed her jacket and the last piece of bacon on the plate.

"Ghezze" she thought out loud as she munched on the piece of bacon and ran out the door.

"Aunt Pearl, here we come."

Jeremiah tucked the journal he had been reading in his coat pocket and got into the driver's seat. Soon maybe Aunt Pearl would be able to give them some information about what was really happening. She seemed to be the one that both the Captain and Mary confided in. He wanted to find out why these two ghosts had such a past that neither of them could rest.

What was it that made the captain bring him into this after all these years? It was quite clear to him that he was somehow an integral piece in the Captains plan. What was that plan though?

The house had been a curse that had been placed on both him and his brother since their youth.

When their mother inherited the house she was thrilled to leave her deadbeat husband behind and bring her two boys to live in Ravenswood Manor. It was exciting to have a mansion passed down to her through family. The fact that her family had basically stolen the home from the Ravenswood family had no effect on her whatsoever. She was a Wentworth and this house was the status of wealth that she desired.

There were stories passed down that it was haunted but she promptly ignored them. It was a mansion after all and it belonged to her. The first night he and his brother spent there the Captain had appeared to them. They both hid under the covers too scared to even peek out. They were sure that the ghost Captain was going to kill them. Night after night he returned just after their mother put them to bed.

He seemed lonely and would sit and tell them stories long after their mother was asleep.

They promised to keep the secret but it didn't take long before his younger brother blabbed to his friends and one thing led to another. Thinking his brother was having a nervous breakdown from her divorce their mother packed up everything and took them away.

Something kept calling him back though compelling him to return to the house.

Beau never spoke of the Captain again, finally telling their mother that Jeremiah had made it all up and that he just went along with it. He had probably even convinced himself of that too. Jeremiah had asked his mother for the house a million times but her reply was that she would burn the house to the ground before she would give it to him especially after what he had done to his brother. As a graduation present she presented the house to Beau.

All he wanted was the money he could get from it but the Captain always chased the buyers away.

It was quite a surprise to him that Beau had even walked into the house to show it to Ali. He swore he would never set foot in it again.

When his brother told him he had a buyer that wanted to restore it, Jeremiah had jumped at the opportunity to do it. He even went as far as finding out that Eddie was the person who handled all her affairs. All he had to do was convince Ali that the house was worth the effort. If he told her the truth about the Captain maybe just maybe she wouldn't care. So he played the game in hopes that she would buy it and then run when the Captain appeared. He could buy it cheap from her and the house would be his. What he didn't expect was the way that the Captain was reacting to Ali. There was something missing and he had to find out what it was. It was as if the Captain had drawn Ali there on purpose, but why? She was not afraid either. It baffled him. She actually came back to the house.

It was as if she wanted to know the truth as much as he did.

They walked into the parlor where Aunt Pearl was sitting rocking in her chair.

"Well, I see you brought a guest with you today Ali? Is that really you Jeremiah?"

"You know Jeremiah?"

"Oh yes, it has been a very long time though. You were just a small boy who loved tall ships if I remember right. Your mother brought you and your brother here from Delaware wasn't it?"

Jeremiah didn't like the way this thing was going. He wanted questions answered not secrets revealed about his life.

"Possibly, I am not sure. My mother had a habit of moving around a lot. I did like tall ships though. A child's dream of being a pirate you know?"

"Yes, a pirate."

"Aunt Pearl we really have a few questions we are hoping that you can tell us more about Miss Lizzie."

"As I told you before my dear Miss Lizzie, like her parents was a servant for the Ravenswood family." They came from Ireland along with a couple other families who worked for the both the Ravenswood family and the Wentworth family."

"Really Jeremiah you should tell her about the Wentworth family yourself."

Jeremiah closed his eyes. He knew this was a bad idea but he was hoping for answers regarding the Captain and now he was sure that it was a terrible idea.

"What does she mean Jeremiah? How would you know about the Wentworth's?"

"Because they are his family my dear hasn't he told you? Oh my Jeremiah, I thought for sure you would have been honest with her."

Jeremiah coughed and tried to speak but the look on Ali's face told him she was not going to listen to anything he had to say now.

"Just when were you going to tell me all of this Jeremiah? You asked to come here on a pretense to learn what? Where a treasure is hidden or something to that effect? Is that it? This is all a great big treasure hunt at my expense? "

"Tell me how did you get the fake ghosts to appear?"

"It's not like that at all Ali, nothing like that at all. Beau is my younger brother. When he said he had a buyer I wanted to find out who it was. I have always wanted the house but my mother despised me and gave it to him instead.

I figured like all the rest you would go running when the Captain showed up, but you didn't, you stayed and I had to find out the reasons why. The Captain has always scared off everyone, but not you. It is you he wants and I want to know why."

"Ali, listen to me my dear. Jeremiah is not the enemy. He is just as lost as you are. The Captain has brought the two of you together for a reason. If he believes that you are his Lizzie then maybe you need to be his Lizzie to find out the answers."

"You're trying to tell me that the ghostly Captain and his wife are real?"

"Yes my dear they are as real as you and I. They are living in between the past and the present. Until the mystery is solved they will remain this way."

"The two of you must figure this mystery out together if you ever want to be rid of the ghosts."

"I have to go" Ali barked off. "I am sorry Aunt Pearl I don't mean to be rude."

"It's quite alright my dear. Whenever someone realizes there is more to this world it can be quite disconcerting."

"We have to go together, after all we came together." Jeremiah said.

"Fine, let's go, but don't expect any conversation in the car."

"Ali, I'm sorry really I am. I did not mean to hurt you. I didn't mean to lie. I just wanted to know what it was that he wanted with you. If I told you I was a Wentworth and that Beau was my brother you wouldn't have hired me. I wouldn't have been there when the Captain finally revealed himself to you. If you remember you didn't handle it all that well."

"You're right something drew me here. Maybe it was the Captain, but while we were becoming friends you should have told me the truth."

"I have never been able to trust any man, and now I find that I can't trust you either."

"I won't kick you out at least for now. I need you to do the work but, once it is done, you are gone, and I will sell the house and be rid of the Ravenswood family, and the Wentworth family."

The rest of trip was silent. Jeremiah pulled the SUV into the drive and headed up to the main house.

"Be careful the floors will be slippery." He yelled to her as she stormed away from him.

He had done it now. There was no turning back and he may have to figure out just who this Lizzie was all by him-self. No matter what, he was not going to give up.

Chapter Sixteen

Jeremiah pulled the journal out of his pocket. Well, he had plenty of time to read now. Chances of sleeping tonight were going to be slim. His brain was in overdrive just trying to figure out how he would win back the trust of Ali.

The journal went on about deals that were depending on a certain trip from India. There were some strange entries that had been made by the Captains father. It was almost as if he had made a special contract that didn't include the Wentworth's.

It seems it was the last trip the Captain ever took. The ship supposedly went down somewhere just outside of Indonesia. There was a cryptic telegram that said the job was done.

It seemed strange to him that no one ever mentioned the death of the Captain and his crew the telegram only stated that the ship had gone down and the job was done.

Tomorrow he was going to look up the records at the court house on Lizzie and her family. There had to be some kind of record of their arrival at Ravensport and what happened to them. He would invite Ali but he was pretty sure she would still be mad at him so, he would wait until he could get some answers.

Ali walked up the staircase. Jeremiah had done a fantastic job while she was gone. He didn't deserve all the anger she blasted at him. Why did men feel they had to lie, and cheat, and weave themselves into webs of deceit?

When she reached the second floor she smelled the sweet smell of lilac as if someone had just brought in fresh flowers and placed them in a vase. She followed the smell down the hallway and into the room above the kitchen.

This was the room they said the nursemaid used. This would have been Lizzie's room. She sat on the bed and looked in the mirror that was blackened from age.

Just who were you Lizzie and why is the Captain still searching for you? She pulled out the dresser drawer and something fell from the bottom. It was a small key. What in the world would this small key go to she thought? When she tried to shove the drawer back into the dresser something was stopping it. She pulled it out and there it was a small worn out diary.

"Well, Miss Lizzie I wonder if this belonged to you?" There was a tiny key lock just about the size of the key she had found. Was she surprised? Nope, she was not surprised at all. Obviously Miss Lizzie wanted her to see something and led her there.

She sighed half expecting the Captain to show up, or Mary being angry again at the fact that she was an intruder in her home. She was going to take this diary and head to bed. She would see if the key opened it up and maybe get some insight into the life of Lizzie. Hopefully it would tell her why he keeps insisting on calling her Lizzie.

She laid the diary on the bed and headed into the bathroom to get ready. There was a thump sound as if someone had opened and shut the bedroom door. She grabbed her robe thinking maybe Jeremiah was making sure the house was locked up.

When she walked back into the bed room she glanced on the bed. The diary was gone. Someone had taken it, someone who obviously did not want her to find out the truth about Lizzie. Whoever it was didn't know what kind of person she was that was for sure. She would never let anyone stop her from finding out the truth. She ran out the bedroom door as her slippers went sliding across the newly varnished and waxed floor and down the flight of stairs.

*****

When Ali awoke she looked around. Nothing was familiar to her. The curtains on the windows were a bright red and black paisley print.

They were not exactly something she would have chosen but with everything that was around her it seemed to fit in just fine. She was lying on a small bed with a red and black satin quilt underneath her.

“Someone here has strange taste I must admit.” She voiced out loud.

“I am so glad that you approve my dear.” The voice came out of a darkened corner. He moved from the shadows. He was short and stocky and looked as though he had walked out of a Pirate movie. She tried not to laugh. He had a swashbuckler style about him with a sword at his side. He took a bow, and tipped his grand feathered hat.

“I am always happy to greet a real lady.” He said.

“Jeremiah this is not funny.” She yelled out expecting him to be hiding somewhere close. “What kind of trick are you playing on me?”

"The Jeremiah you are calling for has yet to be born, my dear. Even if he wished to, and he just might, he could not save you."

"So, who are you, and where am I?"

"We are on a journey my dear, the two of us. No one can see, or hear us. But we are here present in this world."

"Oh really," she starts screaming at the top of her lungs.

"Where am I" she hollered out again hoping someone would come and explain what was happening.

"Come look my dear." He said as he pulled back the curtain from the small window. "As you can see we are on a ship at sea."

"You have kidnapped me?" she screamed at him.

"Dearest Ali, did you not want to know about the Captain and Lizzie? I was sure that I heard you right at dear Pearls house last night."

"You were not at Pearls house."

"Ahh, but yes I was. You see Ali, I am Captain John J. Moreland, Pirate esquire" he bowed again. "I am otherwise known as the pirate Captain of the Black Crow that you are so graciously aboard."

"Yes, my dearest Ali, we are on a ship, a time ship so to speak, one that will be revealing to you many things."

"This is the ship that was in the cove. The one that Jeremiah saw last night when we came home isn't it?"

"Not sure my dear, it might have been, did you see it in the cove?"

"No, Jeremiah did."

"Ahh yes, Jeremiah, he is quite a young man you know very talented, and honorable, unlike his brother Beauregard?"

"I have heard your name before." Ali said.

"Really now, someone has spoken of me? That is highly unlikely my dear, highly unlikely."

"No, I am sure someone mentioned your name."

"Well, I did train Masterson Ravenswood and I did know his father. Possibly the Captain mentioned me to you."

"No, it was not him. I have barely spoken to him. Don't worry; I will remember where I heard your name."

"It would not have been within your social status my dear. That is unless of course you were related to any of the woman at the Red Garter on Tocu Island. No you are much too nice to be related to one of those girls."

"No my dear, you fall more into the realm of sweet Lizzie, now there was a true lady unlike Mary the trollop that she was. Her father was worse than most of the lying thieves that I worked with every day.

Everyone thought of Mary Wentworth Ravenswood as the lady of the house, but all of my men knew her well."

"So tell me Captain John, why am I here with you on the "Black Crow?"

"You are here ma lady to see the truth of Ravenswood Manor."

……

Jeremiah awoke the next morning and figured he had better check on Ali. She had been extremely mad at him yesterday and he had to make it up to her.

As he walked past the cove he noticed that the tall ship was gone from last night. He would have to check later to see who it belonged to. A ship that size, well someone had to have seen it, or know who it belonged too. The flag seemed so familiar like he had seen it somewhere before.

He walked in the front door only to find Ali lying at the bottom of the staircase.

"Oh my God" he yelled as he ran to her.

He kneeled on the floor to check her pulse. She was still breathing. He grabbed his cell phone and called for an ambulance.

"Stay with me Ali, don't leave." He begged her as he told the dispatcher what he had found.

The ambulance arrived and soon they raced off to Willow Hospital with Jeremiah closing in fast behind them.

He paced the emergency room floor cursing him-self for not having settled the fight last night. What would have happened to her to cause this? He was sure the Captain knew why had he not come to him to tell him about this when it happened? Surely he didn't want Ali to die.

The doctor came out and motioned for Jeremiah.

"Your friend is currently in a coma. We're not sure of how much head trauma she has suffered yet. There is not much that you can do at this time. We have your number and we will call you if there is any change. I would certainly let her family know what has happened."

Family, he had no idea of who her family was. He would have to contact Eddie and her publisher. Maybe they would know who to contact.

As he walked in the door the Captain was standing in the living room.

"She is quite alright you know."

"Did you do this to her?"

The Captain laughed. "No Jeremiah I would not have done this to her. I care deeply about her. After all she is my sweet Lizzie."

"She is not Lizzie."

"So you keep saying my boy."

"There was a tall ship last night in the cove. What do you know of that?"

"What flag was flying my boy?"

"I couldn't tell it looked like a bird though."

The captain tilted his head. "Well that is quite interesting."

"What do you mean?"

"Captain John J Moreland, a scoundrel that is for sure."

"Are you telling me a ghost ship belonging to a pirate was in the cove last night?"

"Sounds like it. Strange, not sure why that old coot would take a journey back here."

The captain sat down in his leather chair and lit up his pipe.

"Interesting, this is all very interesting."

*****

"Quick Lizzie, get off the floor hurry before mum sees that you slid down her banister again. She will whoop you for sure."

Ali shook her head. What a fall that was she thought as she stood up rubbing the back of her head. It took her a while to gather her thoughts as she stood at the bottom of the staircase.

Where did all these people come from she thought as people dressed in old fashioned clothes whooshed back and forth in front of her face?

"Lizzie, come on. Mum will be here any minute and we have to be gone."

"Coming Masti" suddenly there was a little girl standing in front of her.

Who are these children playing in my house Ali thought and what the heck is going on?

She tried to stop one of the people running around but her hand went right through them. “Am I dead? Am I a ghost?” She asked herself. “Why is it no one can see or hear me?”

Then she heard his voice from behind her.

“I told you my dear, you are present but they cannot hear you. We are between worlds; the present and the past are jumbled together. What you see before you are fragments in time.”

“Our journey will take us too many places and many times. You will get used to it.”

“Let’s go, we have a lot to see.”

*****

“What are you saying Captain?”

"I am not sure Jeremiah. Captain Moreland was a pirate and a scoundrel but his appearance here and now has to have some kind of meaning. He always admired my Lizzie but I do not know why he would steal her like this."

"She is in the hospital Captain in a coma; she is not with this pirate."

"This is where you are wrong my boy, she is definitely with him. I can feel it."

"If that is true than how do we rescue her?"

"Good question, I have to think. Maybe Pearl can help?"

Before Jeremiah could say Pearl, the captain had vanished.

"I hate it when he does that."

Jeremiah grabbed her purse and started searching for phone numbers to call.

"Hey Ali, you haven't called in days I was beginning to get worried."

"Ahh Eddie, this is Jeremiah. I am afraid something has happened to Ali and we need to get in touch with her family."

"What do you mean?"

"Well, she fell down the staircase at the house and she is in a coma in the hospital."

"What? How did that happen? I have to call Cat right now."

"Well, if you have numbers for her family you should call them. I don't know how long she will remain in this coma. The doc is hoping it won't be long but said he can't tell. Her vitals are strong and that's all in her favor right now."

"We will be on our way." Jeremiah wasn't sure he wanted Eddie there but he was Ali's only real friend and maybe his voice would bring her out of the coma.

Evening had come and the Captain had not returned. Jeremiah decided he would head back to the hospital to check on Ali. There wasn't anything he could do there, but sitting around the house waiting for answers from a ghost was not getting him anywhere either.

He walked into the room and sat next to the bed.

She stood at the end of the bed watching him watch her. It gave her a weird feeling.

"I am here Jeremiah" she said to him putting her hand on his shoulder.

"Why can't he hear me? How do I get back?" she asked.

"You have to see it all before you can return. You have to know the real truth about Captain Ravenswood. He is trapped and only you can release him."

"I don't understand."

"You will soon my dear."

To be continued…..

Thank you for taking the time to read

The Captains Love – Book 1 in my new series

Ravenswood Manor

Journey to Redemption – Book 2 will be coming out soon.

I would love for you to visit my website and feel free to leave me a message about what you thought of my newest series.

Your comments are always welcome.

You can also check out the other books I have written at my Facebook website.

https://www.facebook.com/bkovatchbooks/?ref=aymt_homepage_panel

ABOUT THE AUTHOR

Beverly Kovatch is an Administrative Assistant by trade, a writer by heart, a mother of three, and a grandmother of eight. She has loved writing since she was thirteen, at which time she could be found sitting alone creating short stories, believing one day she would be a sit com writer for a massive television studio.

Reality set in as a young adult when she took a break from her writing dream to raise her family. If she had only realized that life is the story she may have been a successful writer by now. The stories she now creates are the essence of a life filled with love, happiness, tragedy, and regret. She now knows that with every moment given there is a story to share, a life to share it with, and a message of hope to never give up on a dream.

Made in the USA
Columbia, SC
27 April 2017